THE LOST ISLAND

ISLAND

904 000 00608330

Books by Laura Powell

The Last Duchess: A Silver Service Mystery

The Lost Island: A Silver Service Mystery

THE LOST ISLAND

LAURA POWELL

A SILVER SERVICE MYSTERY

ILLUSTRATED BY SARAH GIBB

MACMILLAN CHILDREN'S BOOKS

First published 2018 by Macmillan Children's Books
an imprint of Pan Macmillan
20 New Wharf Road, London N1 9RR
Associated companies throughout the world
www.panmacmillan.com

ISBN 978-1-5098-0892-2

1 3 5 7 9 8 6 4 2

A CIP catalogue record for this book is available from
the British Library.

Printed and bound by CPI Group (UK) Ltd, Croydon CR0 4YY

For Tasnim, Isaac's treasured Dadi,

with love and thanks

A Short Guide to Domestic Servants

The Steward
The steward is in charge of household and estate management. He is not considered a servant in the conventional sense, and is the trusted right hand of the master or mistress.

The Butler
The butler is the principal male servant. His duties include arranging the dining table, carving the meat, serving the wine and attending to the needs of the family and their guests in the dining and drawing rooms. The silverware, cellars and pantries are in his charge.

The Housekeeper
The housekeeper is the principal female servant, and second in command to the butler. She is in charge of the accounts, the tradesmen's bills, the orderly running of the house and the provision of general supplies. She is also responsible for the servants' quarters.

The Valet
The valet attends the master of the household. His duties include keeping his master's wardrobe in order, preparing his bath, shaving him and tidying his dressing room.

The Lady's Maid
The lady's maid waits on the mistress of the household, assisting with her dress and toilette, washing the most delicate items of her wardrobe and using her dressmaking

skills to create and repair clothes. In addition, the lady's maid prepares beauty lotions, and styles her mistress's hair.

The Footman

The footman sets the table for meals and assists the butler, answers the door and attends to various other tasks in the house, such as lighting candles and lamps, polishing silver and cleaning shoes and boots.

The Housemaids

There are several housemaid positions, including parlour maids, chambermaids and laundry maids. Each has their own set of duties, such as lighting fires, bringing up hot water for washing, emptying and cleaning chamber pots, cleaning all the public rooms of the house, making beds, brushing carpets and beating rugs, and washing clothes and linen.

The Cook and Kitchen Maids

The cook is responsible for the kitchen and the provision of meals. She will not do any general cleaning, and her ingredients will mostly be prepared for her by her kitchen maids. Their duties also include lighting the kitchen fires early in the morning.

The Hall Boy

As the lowest ranked male servant, the hall boy's duties include emptying chamber pots for the higher-ranking servants, running errands and cleaning boots.

The Coachman

The stables are supervised by the coachman who also drives the coach, assisted by the **groom** and **stable boy** who also look after the horses.

Lady Hawk's Household

The Hosts
Lady Cecily Hawk
Miss Cassandra Hawk

The Guests
Lord Anthony Charnly
Captain Henry Vyne
The Reverend Frederick Blunt
Mr Thomas Ladlaw
Lady Sylvia Lane, Dowager Duchess of Wenbury
Miss Alicia Lane
Miss Adele Lane
Miss Honoria Blunt
Miss Marian Smith

The Servants
Mr Grey	Steward
Mr Perks	Butler
Mrs Robinson	Housekeeper

Miss Jenks	Lady's Maid to Lady Hawk
Mr Stokes	Valet to Lord Charnly
Alfred	First Footman
William	Second Footman
Jane	Head Housemaid
Elsie	Second Housemaid
Penny (Pattern)	Third Housemaid
Mrs Palfrey	Cook
Ellen	Kitchen Maid
Mabel	Kitchen Maid
Anne	Laundry Maid
Tilly	Scullery Maid
Nathaniel	Hall Boy
James	Coachman
Jacob	Groom

CHAPTER ONE

In commencing a new service, determine to do your duty in it.

S. & S. Adams, *The Complete Servant* (1825)

The crescent of houses was unrelentingly regular and forbiddingly handsome. It seemed more like a wall of battlements than a fashionable terrace.

London itself had the air of a city under siege. A thick, damp fog had invaded its streets, and at seven o'clock on a chilly February evening even the warmth of lit windows failed to pierce the gloom. Anyone who

had the means or opportunity to stay indoors was doing so.

A wraith appeared from within the fog; something insubstantial and pale, which seemed to float along the shrouded street. Close to, it was only a girl – a mere slip of a thing: plainly dressed, light-footed and carrying a shabby carpet bag. She paused to appraise number twenty with a briskness different to her otherwise mousy appearance.

Her name was Pattern, and she was presenting herself for service as housemaid at the residence of Lady Cecily Hawk, London's most celebrated society hostess. In her real identity, as Pattern Pendragon, Countess of Annwn, her arrival should have been met with bowing and scraping footmen and the best reception room in the house. As her reward for saving the life of the Grand Duchess of Elffinberg, she had been promoted from lady's maid to aristocrat. She was now not only one of the noblest personages in Elffinberg – she was also the dearest friend of its young ruler.

Yet here was a curious thing: although Pattern had been exceedingly happy to escape the lot of a domestic drudge, she had not found a life of ease to be entirely to her satisfaction either. Without purpose or challenge, she felt her wits grow dull, and her spirit restless. And so, after unravelling a mystery that had threatened the Grand Duchess (involving a dragon among many other perils!), she had acquired a new employer. It was an investigative agency known as the Silver Service, who numbered her among their most promising recruits, and it was under their direction that, in the guise of plain Penny Pattern, an orphan servant girl, she was now taking the narrow steps down to the tradesman's entrance to number twenty.

She had not been sent here merely to sweep floors and set fires. Evil deeds were rumoured to take place in this household, and it was Pattern's task to uncover them, reporting back to the man who had knocked on the door of the Silver Service because, for all his wealth and power, he had nowhere else to turn.

*

Sir William Whitby was as fine a gentleman as one could wish, with a pink well-fed face and a hearty manner. He was a Member of Parliament and had a large estate in Wiltshire. He also had a ward, Henry: his late cousin's child.

Henry was the cause of his present trouble. Since coming of age, the young man had acquired a taste for drinking and gambling. Last summer, Sir Whitby had dispatched him on a Grand Tour of Europe in the hope that time spent in the appreciation of classical antiquities and Renaissance art would be as morally improving as it was educational. At first, his plan seemed to have succeeded. Henry's letters home were full of the joys of archaeological explorations. He was making connections, furthermore, with the cream of European society. In his last communication, he had mentioned that he was on his way to visit an island near Capri, as the guest of the Contessa Cecelia di Falco and her daughter Cassiphone, one of the most eligible heiresses in Rome. But that was the last anyone had heard of him. Henry had vanished.

Sir Whitby engaged a private investigator to try to discover the fate of his ward. The man tracked down both the servants and the other guests at the Contessa di Falco's house party, all of whom claimed to have no knowledge of Henry. However, their recollections of their island stay were curiously vague. The investigator reported that their accounts of what little they *did* remember were so similar it was almost as if they were reciting lines from a play. Taking matters into his own hands, Sir Whitby travelled to Rome to meet with the Contessa himself. Yet after a whole morning spent in the Contessa's palazzo, Sir Whitby failed to remember what, exactly, had transpired. Although he was sure the Contessa had been entirely charming, he struggled to recall her appearance and dress, let alone their conversation. His only abiding memory of the encounter was of the Contessa's little pug dog, which had lifted its leg against his boot as he'd made his farewell. Sir Whitby felt himself – there was no other word for it – *entranced*.

Sir Whitby returned home very downcast. He was

now certain that Henry had met with an unhappy end, but discovering the true circumstances of his disappearance seemed a hopeless task. For several months, he lost himself in grief. Then that autumn, just over a year after Henry's disappearance, word spread of a glamorous new arrival on the London scene. Lady Cecily Hawk was a wealthy foreign-born widow with a beautiful daughter, Cassandra. An invitation to one of Lady Hawk's salons or soirées quickly became the most sought-after prize in town. Her daughter was besieged by a host of suitors. Furthermore, Lady Hawk was known to have acquired a private island off the Cornish coast. A favoured few were invited there for a house party in March.

Having no clear memory of his encounter with the Contessa, Sir Whitby would never have made a connection between her and Lady Hawk had he not bumped into the lady herself at the opera. Even then, he admitted it was unlikely that he would have recognized her, were it not for the little pug dog that her daughter carried in her arms. *That* piddlesome creature was unmistakable! At once, Sir Whitby was seized by the strange conviction that Lady Hawk and the Contessa di Falco were one and the same. In which case, how had she managed to befuddle him so completely in Rome? How was she involved in Henry's disappearance, and to what end? Was it possible there was something profoundly amiss with the fascination she and her daughter exerted?

Sir Whitby was very uncomfortable in relating this narrative to the Silver Service agency. A man of his rank was not in the habit of consulting servants, unless it was to enquire of his butler which claret was to be brought up from the cellar, or to quiz his valet on the knotting of cravats. Yet here he was, confiding the most painful secrets of his household to people who, in the normal order of things, should barely be seen or heard!

Mr Crichton, director of the Silver Service, had served as butler to some of the highest families in the land, and his colleague Mrs Jervis had been housekeeper to the same. As such, they were entirely sympathetic to the delicate sensibilities of their clients. The Silver

Service was a place of last resort. People found their way to it when mysteries could not be solved by rational means, or when dark magic was hinted at with hushed tones and grave looks. But few knew what to expect when they visited the quiet office by Bedford Square. Only the emblem on the door – a feather duster crossed with a toasting fork – gave any hint as to what kind of business was undertaken within.

Once inside, there was a pleasing scent of clean linen and beeswax, and the atmosphere of orderly calm that is found in all the best-run households. In such a setting, it was hard to imagine the terrors of black magic and creatures of the night. Yet these were the Service's speciality. If you suspected your steward was embezzling funds or that your beloved was not constant with her affections, there was – as Sir Whitby could attest – no shortage of private investigators to take up your case. The Silver Service, however, dealt exclusively with the uncanny. Their business was the stuff of nightmares and bloodthirsty legends; shadowy forces that still lingered from ancient days.

'For who,' Mr Crichton liked to say, 'is better placed than a servant? The perfect servant is the invisible one. Invisible, incorruptible. A trusted servant has access to their employer's most intimate areas of life and work. A clever servant can turn this access to great advantage.'

Mr Crichton was upright and silver-haired, a man who knew how to soften his natural authority with the sheen of deference. Mrs Jervis had the air of everyone's favourite grandmother. These two were the public faces of the Service. The agents working on the ground were generally kept out of sight, their identities hidden to avoid detection. Thus while Pattern was privy to Sir Whitby's visit to the office, watching and listening from a concealed antechamber, the peer would never meet her in person, or even know her name. Perhaps this was just as well – his confidence in the Service would have been sorely tested had he known the fate of his ward was in the hands of a thirteen-year-old housemaid.

'One of our most impressive recruits,' Mrs Jervis told him. 'Whilst in service to foreign royalty, she foiled an attempt to usurp the throne, uncovering

an exceptionally devilish plot.'

At her spy-hole, Pattern frowned. It was true that her time as lady's maid to Her Royal Highness Arianwen Eleri Charlotte Louise, Grand Duchess of Elffinberg, had been of a peculiarly eventful nature. But she always felt a little uncomfortable having attention drawn to her exploits.

Sir Whitby, however, looked decidedly more cheerful at the mention of royalty. If the crowned heads of Europe sought the Service's assistance, then perhaps employing their expertise could be seen as a mark of distinction, rather than something to be kept quiet at all costs.

'Rest assured,' Mr Crichton told him, 'the matter will have our first attention. Lady Hawk or the Contessa di Falco, or whoever she may be, will not be able to hide her true designs for long.'

And so it was settled that Pattern should be placed as a maid in Lady Hawk's establishment. The original third housemaid was persuaded to give sudden notice in return for a generous pay-out, and Pattern was furnished with references by a grateful client of the Service (whose home had been exorcised of a poltergeist). An interview was arranged with the housekeeper a mere three days before the entire servantry was due to depart for Lady Hawk's Cornish estate, where she would be hosting a large party.

As Pattern descended the steps to the tradesman's entrance of Lady Hawk's town house, she felt a tingle in her blood she had not felt since she had crept up a stony Elffish mountainside, poker in hand, as the sky swarmed with stars, and a dragon's breath tarred the air.

She would never have thought that any position could be more daunting than her sudden promotion to lady's maid, when she had been packed off at a moment's notice to serve royalty in a foreign land. This time, she had an even greater weight of expectation on her shoulders.

Since leaving Elffinberg and joining the Service, she had spent most of her time in training, both practical

and theoretical. She had studied previous assignments taken on by the Service, and learned everything she could from them concerning black magic and monsters, not to mention the more practical arts of sabotage, subterfuge and skulduggery. Her poker-fencing skills were now as advanced as her bonnet-trimming, and she could concoct a drug to temporarily paralyse all ten fingers and thumbs as easily as she could mix a common sleeping draught. Pattern's hopes of putting these new talents to the test were accordingly high.

She was determined to be worthy of the Silver Service's confidence in her. A niggling voice liked to whisper that her success in Elffinberg had mostly been a matter of luck. If her investigation of Lady Hawk was successful, then surely the voice of doubt would be silenced once and for all.

In truth, Pattern was almost more wary of her fellow servants than the villainy of their employer. She might be Pattern Pendragon, the girl who had slain a monster and befriended a princess, but she was still young, and shy, and nervous of making her way in an unfamiliar household.

For the moment, however, no surprises or alarms lay in wait for her behind the back door. Pattern was shown through very civilly to the housekeeper's room, where she was asked about her former positions and training, and watched carefully as she recited the dates and names. Mrs Robinson had clearly taken the previous housemaid's desertion hard.

'To leave to nurse a sick aunt, of all people! If it were a parent, one might understand – but only an *aunt* . . .' She examined Pattern through her spectacles. 'Pardon me, but you are very small for fifteen. I would never have taken you for being such a grown girl.'

Pattern was fairly small for thirteen too. It was something she tried not to let bother her. 'Please, ma'am, I may be small, but I am strong.'

Mrs Robinson sighed. 'Well, we cannot afford to be choosy so late in the day.'

She explained that Lady Hawk and her daughter were presently staying with friends while their servants shut up the house. The island property in Cornwall was

stocked with all the provisions the party would require, so there was little to pack except the ladies' wardrobes, and their own personal effects. But the town house must still be cleaned from top to bottom, its valuables secured and its rooms shrouded in dust sheets.

'In your letter of recommendation, it says that you are a quick learner – and so shall we all need to be. The Cornish property is new to us servants, and I fear we are rather a small staff to host such a large gathering, and in such a place . . .' She caught herself. 'But I am assured everything there is in excellent order. Our mistress is a very gracious and kindly lady, and generous to a fault.'

Whatever evil schemes Lady Hawk might be concocting, Pattern thought it was to her credit that she did not exploit her staff. In fact, so far the only unusual thing that had been discovered about the lady was that both she and her daughter were vegetarians, which, although eccentric, was hardly criminal.

The second housemaid showed Pattern to their shared attic room. Elsie was a pink-cheeked girl of about eighteen, and as chatty and unquestioning as

Pattern could have hoped. Elsie confided that the butler, Mr Perks, was a stickler for the dusting, but wasn't a bad sort on the whole; that Alfred, the first footman, fancied himself a ladies' man; and that when she was in a good humour, Mrs Palfrey, the cook, would give them the off-cuts from her pastry-making. She also assured Pattern that, despite the Hawk ladies' unusual diet, meat was served to their servants as well as their guests.

Pattern nodded and smiled. At this stage, all information was useful. She had already studied the list of her fellow servants and so knew their names if not their character. The upper servants were Mr Perks, the butler; Mrs Robinson, the housekeeper; and Mrs Palfrey, the cook. Then there were the first and second footmen, Alfred and William; James, the coachman; Jacob, the groom; and Nathaniel, the hall boy. The female domestics were the kitchen maids, Ellen and Mabel; Tilly, the scullery maid; Anne, the laundry maid; and then the housemaids, Jane, Elsie and herself. Miss Jenks, Lady Hawk's maid, was currently

accompanying her mistress on her visit.

'When I started, I was afeared we'd all be worn ragged,' Elsie confided. 'There may only be two ladies to look after, but the missus is a great one for entertaining, make no mistake, and hardly a day goes by without a crowd of gentlemen calling for the young miss, or a whist party or supper or a dance. So you'd expect there to be a deal of work, but, truth be told, somehow it doesn't add up to all that much. Jane was saying just this morning there's times she fancies the house almost cleans itself!'

Pattern knew that gossip was her first and best resource, but encouraging it did not come easily. People assumed she must be a very serious person, partly because she had more schooling than most girls of her kind, but also because of her natural reserve. She tried to match Elsie's prattling manner.

'Is the young lady, Miss Hawk, as lovely as they say?'

'Wait till you see her! Like a little doll, she is. Peaches and cream and curls of gold. I should think half the gentlemen in the country are in love with her.'

'Perhaps they find her foreign ways refreshing.'

'Oh no,' said Elsie, looking somewhat shocked by the notion. 'Miss Hawk is as fine and proper an English lady as ever there was.'

'But I heard the mistress has been living overseas?'

'I s'pose she *does* have something a touch "continental" about her,' Elsie admitted. 'They've done a deal of travelling, anyhow. Paris, I think, and that city where they make the pastries, and somewhere with mountains, and someplace else with lakes . . . And now we're to journey to distant parts ourselves! I'm not sure what to think of it, myself. People say Cornwall is full of the queerest things: pirates and mermaids and the like.'

In normal circumstances, Pattern might have laughed. Pirates and mermaids, indeed! But after her own adventures, who knew what strange encounters might be awaiting them?

CHAPTER TWO

The best proof of wisdom is to talk little, but to hear much.

S. & S. Adams, *The Complete Servant*

Pattern disliked muddle and fuss. She feared never growing any taller, the London Omnibus and dragons. What she was *not* afraid of was hard work. Which was useful for her first challenge: how to pass as an experienced housemaid. She had not emptied slops or beaten carpets since her time at Mrs Minchin's Academy of Domestic Servitude, where she had been top of the class, and so quickly graduated to less irksome chores. After her unprecedented promotion to lady's maid, her duties – dragon slaying aside – had been even more refined.

Lady Hawk's domestics were well paid, the food was plain but plentiful, the servants' quarters were not excessively draughty, and her mattress only had a couple of lumps in it. But, as the third housemaid, Pattern would be working fifteen-hour days of hard labour. She had got used to a life of feather beds and silk stockings more quickly than she would have thought possible.

She was reminded of this the morning of her second day of work. She was below stairs looking for more scouring paper for the grates when a lad around her own age peeped out of the doors of the boot room.

'You the new girl? I'm the hall boy, Nate.'

'Penny,' said Pattern. 'Pleased to meet you.'

Nate had an easy smile and air of confidence that she rather envied. His dark skin was in contrast to the pale and pasty faces of his fellow servants, but the most significant difference about him, Pattern thought, was the very sharp look he had in his eyes.

'Same to you,' he said. 'Where d'you spring from?'

The Silver Service had provided Pattern with an account of her working life that was as dull as it was conventional; Mrs Robinson had found it entirely satisfactory, and she assumed Nate would as well.

Yet when she'd finished her history, the hall boy whistled. 'Coo! I thought *this* place was cushy. But I ain't never seen an ex-scullery maid with hands like yours.'

Pattern coloured despite herself. She had bitten down her nails as part of her preparations, but the skin on her hands was still relatively smooth, not cracked and red from months of scrubbing dirty pans. Fortunately, Nate's attention soon moved on. He, along with the rest of the servantry, was excited about the trip to Cornwall, and eager to share his hopes for the party.

'I reckon there's good tips to be made, on account of all the gentlemen wanting their boots extra shiny to go courting.'

Pattern understood that the guests included Miss Hawk's most favoured suitors, as well as her high-society friends. 'Everyone keeps telling me Miss

Hawk's the toast of London.'

'I don't see what all the fuss is about myself. One of them milk-and-water types.'

Pattern, who had herself been described as 'milk and water', as well as 'mousy' on occasion, wondered if Miss Hawk was similarly misunderstood. It could be useful to be underestimated. However, her chief concern for the moment was Miss Hawk's mama. 'I'm sure having her daughter so admired must be a comfort to the mistress. Seeing as she's a widow, and has spent so many years away.'

'Well, the missus can't have been very sentimental about her husband, whoever he was. Ain't no sign of him around the shop. Even the—'

The stately tread of Mr Perks, the butler, was heard on the stairs. Nate immediately vanished into the boot room. Pattern rubbed her aching back, and hastened off to her grate-polishing. Elsie might have said that the house cleaned itself, but Pattern was yet to see evidence of such a miracle.

She saw no evidence of Lady Hawk's late husband,

either, let alone Sir Whitby's missing ward. The house's furnishings were handsome and costly, but there was little indication of individual taste. As she worked her way through the rooms, Pattern was disappointed to find no portraiture or keepsakes, let alone journals or letters that might shed light on the lady's past exploits or future intentions. She and her daughter had left no trace of personality behind them.

On her last night in London, Pattern went to collect correspondence that the Silver Service had forwarded to her, under care of a grocer's in Grantham Green. She was presented with a somewhat sticky package of gingerbread, sent by Dilys, once housemaid at the Castle of Elffinberg, now promoted to keeper of the royal wardrobe. The gingerbread was accompanied by a bulletin of below-stairs gossip, which Pattern struggled to follow, but was very glad to receive. There was also a very long, very affectionate letter from the Grand Duchess, full of exclamations and underlining, and written in a variety of coloured inks.

The mere sight of this exuberant penmanship was enough for Pattern to feel a surge of homesickness for Elffinberg. It was still a marvel to her that she should have such a friend. They had begun as mistress and maid, and the Grand Duchess was no easy employer, irritable, excitable and prone to all kinds of madcap schemes. But once Pattern had discovered the hidden dangers that beset her young mistress, the Grand Duchess's eccentricities became easy to understand. Understanding grew into mutual respect, and then to true and deep affection. They had vanquished monsters together – both human and beast – and each considered the other a sister of the heart.

'. . . *It is still a Great Mystery why you should choose to toil away in such a disagreeable and dangerous fashion, when we could be having a perfectly <u>delightful</u> time together here in Elffinberg. Hardly any sort of fun is to be had without you! Now, I know that you are Excessively Sensible, as well as terribly clever, but whatever Unpleasantness you get mixed up in next, you <u>must</u> take very <u>great care</u>, and remember <u>how much</u> I am counting on you for all manner*

of things. My new maid, Morris, is Fearfully Dull (she has not a tenth of your way with ringlets!), and, furthermore, I suspect the Finance Minister of muddling his sums. Is it not extraordinary how these learned gentlemen can be such dunderheads? Dearest Pattern, you must <u>make haste</u> to finish whatever Heroics you are undertaking, and come home and set us all to rights . . .'

Pattern had explained to Eleri as much about the Service as she was able, but she was not able to relate the details of Sir Whitby's case. So her reply was devoted to answering Eleri's various questions and complaints rather than conveying any real news of her own. She felt rather worn out by the time she was finished. From here on, the only letters she would write would be to Mr Crichton and Mrs Jervis. They would be addressed to a fictitious sister, relating Pattern's progress using various coded references. But this was assuming the Isle of Cull had the facility to dispatch letters. It was quite possible that, once there, Pattern would be without any means of communication with the outside world.

*

The journey from London to Cornwall, made with the other servants in public stagecoaches under the watchful eye of Mrs Robinson, was long and arduous. When they finally arrived at the fishing village from where they were to take the four-mile boat journey to Cull, Pattern was so cramped and stiff she felt she would almost be glad to get back to scrubbing grates and mopping floors.

Elsie had not stopped chattering since they had left London. Everything was new; everything was of interest. Pattern had sympathy for this – she had been just as wide-eyed on *her* first escape from the city. However, she had kept her astonishment to herself. Elsie could not pass sight of a cow, or a stream, or a picturesque cottage without remarking on it – and the moment she and the other maids caught sight of the sea there was a hubbub to rival even the noisiest gull. Not even Mrs Robinson's stern admonishments could silence them.

It was not the best of days for a visit to the coast. The fog seemed to have followed them from London,

and everything was dank, dripping and smelling of fish. Pattern – already somewhat sick from the jolting of the coach – looked at the choppy grey expanse of water and felt queasier still. She reflected that the Service had been advised that Cull was a craggy and desolate place. The fisherman who was to ferry them over would only shrug in response to Pattern's enquiries about the island's history.

'Loss,' was all he would volunteer.

'Who is lost?' she asked. His accent was so thick, and his manner so brusque, she feared she had misheard him.

'*Cull*. 'Tis from the Cornish for "loss".'

The Isle of Loss . . . This did not bode well. Pattern was not a fanciful girl, but she shivered all the same.

Yet when the shores of Cull first rose out of the mist, Pattern gaped in admiration just like the other girls. Although the island's cliffs were rocky, they were fringed thickly by trees, and the cove they were approaching glittered with white sand. The waves that lapped the island were a deep blue-green, not grey.

Except, that is, for the sea immediately ahead of their

vessel. Pattern thought the black mass beneath the water must be submerged rocks, but then the darkness moved, passing under the boat like an underwater shadow. A few dirty bubbles rose to the surface. Nobody else had noticed it, and Pattern herself could not be sure of what she had seen.

Then all at once the last of the clouds parted and the sun blazed through, so that the scene before them was bathed in golden light, and the remaining mist that enveloped the isle was transformed into a sparkling, shimmering haze.

CHAPTER THREE

The fishermen drew the boat up to a stone pier and helped them disembark on to the landing platform at the end. An old man, swathed in a billowing black cloak, was waiting to receive them at the top of the steps.

'My name is Glaucus Grey, and I am the steward of this isle. On behalf of Lady Hawk, I am pleased to welcome you to Cull.' He gave a stiff little bow. Some of the more impertinent maids smirked at his appearance. He had bristly white eyebrows and a wild white mane of hair, and a face that was exceedingly knobbly. But he hobbled across the beach very briskly, and it was quite a struggle to keep up with him as they hauled their baggage up the rough steps cut into the cliff face.

At the top of the steps, Pattern paused to take a breath. When she glanced back, she saw the boat that had brought them was already swallowed up by mist. Yet the sun continued to shine on Cull as the party followed a path through a wood. On the other side of a narrow though not particularly deep ravine was a sheltered glade dappled with snowdrops.

Elsie, naturally, stopped and stared. 'What pretty flowers! Like little stars!'

'The local name for them is the moly flower – but they're for looking at, no more,' cautioned the steward. 'That side of the wood is dangerous, and strictly out of bounds.'

Mrs Robinson peered across. 'But it looks such a charming spot.'

The old man grunted. 'You've heard of the Cornish adder, perhaps. Well, the Cull viper is its more vicious cousin. It nests up here, in that very glade, and a bite from its fangs is fatal. So keep your distance.'

After this warning, all were relieved to leave the wood. Emerging from the trees, they saw an arcaded villa set against the hill. It was classical in style, with ice-cream-pale-yellow walls and a roof of terracotta tiles. A wide lawn in front of the house gave way to a formal garden with flower beds worked into patterns of stars, half-moons and mathematical symbols, broken up by white pebble paths. Statues of nymphs and satyrs peeped out from a tangle of rose bushes.

There was no sign of groundsmen or gardeners, and the place was silent apart from the drone of bees and the sigh of the sea. Even the chattering maids were quiet, too overwhelmed to do anything but stare. As the visitors made their way through the grounds, it felt as if the villa and landscape were half asleep, lying there drugged in the spring sunshine.

'Gracious!' exclaimed Mrs Robinson, surveying the orchard. 'Are those *lemon* trees?'

Mr Grey smiled. 'Cull's positioning is geographically unique. Thanks to a most favourable union of winds and tides, the climate here is considerably warmer and drier than anywhere on the mainland.'

'I see,' Mrs Robinson said rather faintly. 'Am I to understand, Mr, er, Grey, that you have sole charge of the property in Lady Hawk's absence?'

'That is so. I have been in service to my lady for so many years, I can hardly remember a time that I wasn't.'

'And no one else lives on the island?'

'Folk from the village make the crossing to tend to the estate, and deliver such produce we cannot supply ourselves, but none are resident unless stranded here by bad weather.'

'But are there really no other servants? I was under the impression that casual staff would be engaged—'

'My lady is quite satisfied that you will be up to the job.'

Mrs Robinson pursed her lips. The maids exchanged grimaces. Sixteen servants was a large number for a town house. But in a country villa of this size, with a party of guests to look after, they would be sorely stretched.

The aged steward led them through a sunken walled garden, richly scented with herbs, to the service quarters. The rooms were large and echoing, with plaster peeling from the walls, and windows so overgrown with creepers that the place was bathed in a greenish light. In the servants' hall, a bare lofty room with a tiled floor, they were met by Mr Perks, the butler, who had come ahead with Mrs Palfrey and the other domestics and was doing his best to act as if he'd had charge of this strange property his whole working life.

The sleepy silence of the place was soon overwhelmed by noise and bustle. Rooms must be aired, fires laid and beds made, and the contents of cabinets, closets and pantries explored. It was heartening to find the house, though unlived in for so long, was in excellent order. Mr Grey had previously arranged for provisions to be brought to the island by boat, and the larder and wine cellar were well stocked. The meat safe, coal-hole and ice-house were all packed to bursting. Everything from shoe polish to sealing wax was in its proper place.

Lady Hawk and her daughter would be arriving the next morning, the rest of the party the day after. As Pattern set about beating carpets, she rehearsed what she knew of the visitors in her head.

The gentlemen were all suitors of Miss Hawk. The most eligible was Lord Anthony Charnly, heir to a vast estate in Norfolk. His friend and rival Captain Henry Vyne was known as the handsomest man in England – and the best card player in his regiment. The Reverend Frederick Blunt was more of a catch than most young clergymen, thanks to his aristocratic connections and the patronage of his uncle, the Archbishop of Barnchester. The final suitor was a poet, Mr Thomas Ladlaw, who had been favoured by very complimentary notices in the *London Poetical Review*. His fortunes had further improved with a publication of a novel in the Gothic style, *The Towers of Callabrio*.

This much was public knowledge. The Silver Service, however, had been able to dig a little deeper, thanks to its information network of well-placed servants. These sources reported that Lord Charnly had been implicated in the death of an old woman on his estate, though the matter had been hushed up, and the circumstances remained vague. Captain Vyne had left a string of broken hearts in his wake over the years, and was rumoured to have fathered two illegitimate children. The Reverend Blunt was said to have stolen from a charity that he himself had established for the relief of widows and orphans. Only Mr Ladlaw, the poet, appeared clear of wrongdoing.

The visiting group of ladies comprised society favourites Alicia and Adele Lane; their aunt Lady Sylvia Lane, the Dowager Duchess of Wenbury; Frederick Blunt's sister Honoria; and her companion Marian Smith, a poor relation.

Pattern not only had to acquaint herself with the honoured guests, but the servants they would bring with them, though since these servants would be mixing with their fellows below stairs, getting to know them would be easy enough. Pattern's focus must be the gentlemen. The lord, the soldier, the priest and the poet . . . united only in their passionate desire to win Miss Hawk's hand.

London's drawing rooms were abuzz with talk of how Miss Hawk must finally be ready to make her decision. Why else would she gather her most ardent suitors together, and in Cornwall? The charitable view was that she wished to make her choice away from the pressures and distractions of town. The less well-meaning gossips thought that she – or her mama – intended to wring every last drop of drama from the occasion, and so had set up the party as a particularly vulgar competition, with herself as the prize.

Pattern wondered how the other young ladies would feel, being little more than accessories to Miss Hawk's beauty. It could give rise to a certain amount of tension and resentment, she imagined. But then Miss Hawk could only marry *one* gentleman. The disappointed suitors might well seek consolation elsewhere . . .

Sir Whitby had told the Silver Service that he believed Lady Hawk and the Contessa di Falco were one and the same, and that Cassandra Hawk was likewise Cassiphone di Falco. Cassiphone had been one of the most eligible heiresses in Rome; Henry Whitby was only one of several suitors who she had invited to holiday on her mama's island. The similarities with the present set-up on Cull could not be denied.

But, if Henry had in fact been a victim of foul play, it was still *possible* that the crime was of the ordinary sort. Perhaps there had been a young lady whose affections Henry had slighted in favour of Miss Hawk, or a rival suitor who became dangerous in his desperation . . . Either of these could have done him an injury. Perhaps Miss Hawk and her mother had discovered this, and been threatened in some way by the perpetrator. Then, either from fear of danger, or dread of scandal, they had decided to change their identities and leave the whole sorry business behind them. That might explain why Miss Hawk's time in Italy had not resulted in marriage, and why she and her mama had sought to reinvent themselves in London.

Either way, Pattern knew she must try to keep an open mind on Lady Hawk's alleged Dark Arts. Sir Whitby was feeling both grief and guilt over the loss of his ward. His judgement could not be trusted. Yet secretly Pattern hoped for some supernatural peril – to test her wits against common villainy would, Pattern felt, be a waste of her new-found expertise.

At three o'clock sharp, the servantry gathered at the main entrance to the villa, forming a reception line to greet their employer. Only Mr Grey was absent. They were wearing their expensive new livery and arrayed in order of their station. Mr Perks had inspected them three times over to ensure no hair was out of place, no button done crooked, no smudge seen upon a shoe.

A few minutes later, James the coachman could be seen driving the carriage along the winding avenue. After coming to a stop, narrowly avoiding a strutting peacock, Mr Perks hastened to assist the lady and her daughter down from their vehicle. 'Welcome to Cull,

milady.' He proceeded to escort Lady Hawk down the line of servants, in the manner of two generals inspecting the troops.

Lady Hawk had words of greeting for the senior staff, and a gracious smile and a nod for everyone else. She was tall and handsome, with a high arched nose and a great quantity of inky-black hair. Her complexion was enlivened by a pair of brilliant dark eyes and a full red mouth. The contrast to her daughter was striking. Miss Hawk was, indeed, a perfect English rose, as pale and dainty as her mother was bold and dark. She glided behind her with downcast eyes and a sweetly bland expression, holding a little pug dog in her arms.

Lady Hawk's maid, Miss Jenks, waited by the carriage. She was an elegant young person with a haughty expression, and dressed so finely she hardly looked like a servant. Even so, Pattern knew it was in her interests to befriend her. A lady's maid was often privy to her mistress's secrets, as Pattern herself had once been, and even if Miss Jenks had only been with Lady Hawk for a short while she was in a uniquely intimate position.

Then there was Glaucus Grey, the only person to have been in the lady's employ for longer than a few months. He, at least, must know something of her history . . .

Pattern's thoughts were running on so busily, it took a moment to realize that Lady Hawk had stopped in front of her.

'Now, here's a face I do not recognize.'

Pattern bobbed a curtsey. 'Please, milady, I am new to the position. My name is Penny, milady.'

Mrs Robinson stepped forward to explain the original third housemaid's desertion.

'Penny, you say?' Lady Hawk smiled. She had the merest trace of a foreign accent. 'So which of your parents enjoyed a Classical education?'

'I – um – I'm sorry, milady . . . I don't quite—'

'Never mind, child. I'm only teasing. Perhaps you have not heard of the original Penelope: the long-suffering wife of that rascal Odysseus.'

'No, milady.' Pattern had little in the way of a formal

education, least of all a Classical one, though she had endeavoured to make up for this by close study of the *Encyclopaedia Britannica*. She had chosen 'Penny' because it was a shortened form of both Penelope and Pendragon, her newly acquired surname.

Fortunately, Lady Hawk did not pursue the subject. 'Well, I hope you will be happy with us, little Penelope.' She raised her voice to address the rest of the servants. 'Indeed, I hope you will *all* be happy here. A gathering such as this is hard work for everyone, I know. But I am sure we will show our guests every hospitality. They have been chosen with care, and I am determined to give them exactly what they deserve, for my island is a special place. A sacred spot! Serve it well, and it shall reward you.'

The Mistress of Cull might describe the isle as a sacred spot, but it was certainly a very curious one. After all, Pattern reflected, there could not be many woods in England that were both blessed with snowdrops out of season and infested with snakes. But though Lady Hawk seemed to be a somewhat unusual employer her servants thought none the worse of her for it. The good order of the house, and the comfort of their own quarters, had done much to raise their spirits. From the light-hearted chatter that followed the inspection, Pattern realized she was alone in thinking that Lady Hawk's promise to give her guests 'exactly what they deserve' might conceal a note of threat.

CHAPTER FOUR

❧ ❧

It does not invariably happen that persons remain single because they are not worth having, or that others are married because they are.

Mrs Taylor, *Practical Hints to Young Females* (1815)

❧ ❧

Eager as Pattern was to explore the island, her duties confined her to the house, and until she was granted some time off she would have to make the best of whatever she could discover around her.

The villa certainly had more character than the London house. Songbirds in cages chirruped in the mosaic-tiled central courtyard, where a fountain splashed into a marble basin and miniature orange trees scented the air. The drawing room's ceiling was painted with blue skies and cavorting cherubs, and there was a music room with walls covered in frescoes of vines and birds. The furniture was a curious mixture of stolid English pieces, common to any traditional country house, and Classical antiquities – marble busts, clay urns, bronzes of gods and monsters.

'Rum sort of place, ain't it?' remarked Nate, the hall boy, passing Pattern in the upstairs gallery. 'As if we've wandered onstage at the music hall.'

Pattern looked up from the Greek vase she was inspecting. It was black and red, and painted with a very horrid monster, which had six female heads, and twelve tentacles instead of legs. The vase was displayed in an alcove beneath a framed needlepoint tapestry of an English country garden, embroidered with the title 'Home, Sweet Home'.

'What do you mean?' she asked.

'Like we're here as decoration – same as that.' He gestured to the needlepoint. 'Or the billiards table or the toast rack or the copy of *The Times* in the hall. To make it all seem more . . . believable. Because even the sunshine feels different here – foreign. Have you noticed? And that garden! I ain't no gardener, but even I can see there's things growing out there that shouldn't be blooming in England at all, let alone England in March.'

'Yes, it was strange to see snowdrops still flowering in the wood. But I was pleased, too, as they are a favourite of mine.' Pattern was remembering the muddy patch of hedge outside the Academy of Domestic Servitude. A single clump of snowdrops had grown under it each spring, and she had always thought their appearance a miraculous sight. 'Mr Grey did say the climate of Cull is exceptional.'

'He's a mighty strange old cove.' Nate shrugged. 'I dunno. Could be I'm going soft in the head. But I think we'd do well to keep our wits about us.'

Pattern was cheered by this conversation. It felt good

to know she was not, after all, the only person here who felt unsettled by Cull.

The rest of the servantry were mostly preoccupied with Miss Hawk's matrimonial prospects. During preparations for tea, the conversation turned – as it often did, whenever Mr Perks and Mrs Robinson were out of earshot – to gossip about the young lady.

'She's bound to accept one of her suitors by the end of their stay, don't you think?' Elsie pondered aloud. 'Why else would she have got them all down here, with the sea air so wholesome and the views so delightful? I can't imagine a prettier place for a proposal. And then we shall have a wedding to prepare for!' The housemaid looked as delighted by the prospect as if it were her own marriage. 'But however will she chose?'

The other servants were, of course, already acquainted with Miss Hawk's admirers. Nobody liked Lord Charnly, as he was rude and insolent. Captain Vyne was a favourite with the maids, being so handsome, and Nate liked him too, for back in London the Captain

had given him a fistful of coins once just to deliver a letter. Mr Ladlaw also had his champions.

'Such a romantic young man!' Mrs Palfrey said with a sigh. As well as being one of the finest cooks in London, she was of a sentimental bent.

'And it hardly matters he's only a poet,' put in Jane, the head housemaid, more practically, 'because she has wealth enough for both of them.'

By contrast, the clergyman, Reverend Blunt, was deemed far too boring to excite anyone's admiration. 'Imagine,' said Mabel, the younger kitchen maid. 'He'd be preaching sermons at you all day!'

When they had somewhat quietened down, Pattern asked if anyone knew of a Mr Henry Whitby; her cousin was in service to his family, and had told her he was a great admirer of Miss Hawk. She was able to describe him in some detail, since the Silver Service had arranged for her to study his portrait. (Even allowing for the artist's flattery, the young man did not appear particular dashing, being plump and snub-nosed, with somewhat bulging eyes.) In addition to this, she knew he was a bad gambler and heavy drinker, had a passion for oysters, and favoured Portuguese snuff.

But neither his name nor description meant anything to anyone present, and the conversation soon moved to whether Miss Hawk would be likely to favour a wedding gown of silver lamé and white satin, as had been seen in the recent wedding of the Hon. Lucinda Rice to the Marquis of Harlymoor.

If Miss Hawk was capable of feeling as deeply as her suitors did, she certainly hid it well, and Pattern was increasingly curious about what passions might burn under the girl's quiet exterior. Fatigued by their journey, Lady Hawk had said that she and her daughter would take their supper in their rooms, and so Pattern volunteered to help Miss Jenks by delivering the young lady's tray.

She found Miss Hawk already in her nightgown, sitting at her dressing table and combing her hair in front of the mirror. Her curls shone lustrous in the candlelight.

'Thank you,' she said softly, as Pattern laid down the

supper. She did not take her eye off her reflection.

When Pattern came to collect the tray later, the plates were clean. But it looked as if the girl had not moved. She was still sitting at her dressing table, still combing her hair, the same sweet vacant smile on her face.

CHAPTER FIVE

ᕲᕲ ᕲᕲ

Hospitality is a virtue recommended in Scripture.

Mrs Taylor, *Practical Hints to Young Females*

ᕲᕲ ᕲᕲ

Lady Hawk's guests were ferried to the island by a specially chartered boat the next morning, since a fishing vessel would hardly be suitable for such important passengers. Frederick Blunt, the clergyman, escorting his sister and her companion, Miss Smith, arrived with the Lane ladies and their aunt in the morning. The other three gentlemen came after luncheon. Once everyone was assembled, tea was taken on the lawn,

and, given the small number of staff, Pattern and the other housemaids helped to serve it. It was the ideal opportunity to survey the party.

The trestle tables were laid with beautiful lace cloths, and urns of tea steamed gently among tiers of Mrs Palfrey's finest cakes. The young ladies, pale and gauzy in their summer frocks, seemed almost to float upon the grass. Everyone remarked on the glorious weather and the picturesque scene, congratulated themselves on escaping the tedium of town and marvelled that they were a mere four miles from the English coast.

Meanwhile, the servants, sweating in their new livery, scurried back and forth with more tea, more jam, more scented napkins.

Lady Sylvia Lane, the elderly Dowager, did not look likely to be a very fearsome chaperone. Indeed, on sitting down on a wicker chair in the shade, she very soon fell asleep. Her nieces Alicia and Adele were hard to tell apart, with their bouncing ringlets, rosy cheeks and matching trills of laughter. Honoria Blunt was a regal brunette who spoke with authority on any subject, whether *Fordyce's Sermons* or the Lord Mayor's Ball. Only Marian Smith, Miss Blunt's companion, seemed in the doldrums. She was a small, faded-looking person, with red-rimmed eyes, which – so Pattern noticed – were often fixed on Mr Ladlaw.

Pattern knew at once that Mr Ladlaw must be the poet because he so clearly looked the part, with ink-stained fingers, a brooding expression and an unruly shock of dark hair. Lord Charnly was handsome enough, with heavy-lidded eyes and a jutting jaw, but his manner was very rough. Pattern resolved to keep

her distance from him where at all possible; the Silver Service's informants reported that his violent temper had seen him involved in several brawls, and even one rumoured death.

Perhaps the Reverend Blunt was aware of His Lordship's reputation, for he cast him several disapproving looks. However, given the clergyman's history of stealing from his own charity, Pattern did not think he was really in a position to judge. Whereas Reverend Blunt was rather stout and ungainly in appearance, Captain Vyne positively glittered with charm. As fair and dashing as a fairy-tale prince, he winked at Jane, the prettiest of the maids, said something that made Elsie blush and – before she fell asleep – even had the old Dowager aflutter with his smiles and compliments.

Miss Hawk, meanwhile, did nothing but smile and nod and make occasional remarks about the weather. She was dressed in her customary white, her only adornment a gold charm in the shape of a key, which she always wore round her neck, and though she made for a very pretty picture Pattern found it curious that neither the liveliness of the Lane sisters nor the dash of Miss Blunt seemed to make any kind of impression on the gentlemen. If the other ladies were hoping that more than one engagement might result from the party, it looked, for the moment, as though they would be disappointed.

The gentlemen were already well acquainted with each other. For several weeks, they had been scowling at each other at parties, suppers and soirées spent in pursuit of Miss Hawk. Their competitive gallantry towards her, and insincere civility towards one another, set Pattern's teeth on edge.

Perhaps she was not the only person to feel this way.

'Dear me,' said Honoria Blunt, the clergyman's sharp sister, 'there is so much politeness in the air it is rather like breathing in a cloud of powdered sugar.'

'It was certainly very kind of dear Miss Hawk to invite us,' gushed Adele, who, along with her sister, had set upon a strategy of relentless cheerfulness. 'We are such new acquaintances, after all.'

'I am sure that after our stay here,' Alicia trilled, 'we will all be the *best* of friends!'

'Perhaps someone should tell that to the gentlemen,' said Miss Smith, though so quietly the only person to hear her was Pattern.

Miss Hawk's mama came late to tea, emerging from the villa with a magnificent peregrine falcon on her arm. It was wearing a jewelled collar and sat on her shoulder as she fed it tit-bits of iced cake. 'I adore birds and beasts of every kind,' she declared. 'And they learn to love me in return. This is my darling Alphonse. See how docile he is – like a baby! All my pets are.'

Everyone made admiring noises, and the Lane sisters cooed as enthusiastically as if it had been an actual infant. Nonetheless, Alphonse's tawny eyes had an angry glint, and his beak was cruelly sharp. Despite Reverend Blunt claiming a keen interest in ornithology, the only person who took up Lady Hawk's invitation to pet the bird was her daughter.

'O savage majesty, tamed by a fair maiden's hand!' declaimed Mr Ladlaw. 'Lightning-beaked bolt of feathered awe! Cloud-blazoned warrior of wing and claw! How proud his . . . um . . . How swift the . . . er . . .' But faced with Miss Hawk's calm gaze his powers of poetic invention deserted him, and he lapsed into sulky silence.

'D'you hunt with it, my lady?' Lord Charnly enquired. It was the first sign of interest he had shown in anything save for Miss Hawk.

'I confess I have little taste for blood sports.'

'Lord Charnly is a champion huntsman.' Captain Vyne's smile had a malicious glint. 'Foxes, deer and all manner of game. He was saying on the boat that last season he bagged near three thousand pheasants.'

'Whereas *you*, dear Captain,' said Lady Hawk, 'are a hunter of men! I'm sure your feats of daring in battle are immeasurable.'

Now it was Captain Vyne's turn to look uncomfortable. He had yet to see active service, and his time in the army was mostly occupied with drinking and gambling in the Officers' Mess.

The Reverend Blunt seized his chance. 'The Bible

tells us we have much to learn from the animal kingdom. As Our Lord said, "Who teaches us more than the beasts of the earth, and makes us wiser than the fowls of heaven?"' He absent-mindedly helped himself to a cream puff from Miss Smith's plate. 'Ha – I'd certainly rate my horse or my dog above most of my servants. After all, they do their work more faithfully, and with a deal less complaint.'

This was, at least, a subject the rivals could agree on and the ladies contribute to, and so the tea party ended with an animated discussion of the faults and failings of the servant class.

The servants had scarcely finished clearing away the tea when it was time to prepare for dinner. Mr Perks had given them a little speech after prayers that morning on the importance of Pulling Together and Sharing the Load, with additional remarks on the virtues of Industry, Fidelity, Diligence and Calm. However, both he and Mrs Robinson wore a distinctly harassed air, and Mrs Palfrey's kitchen had been a whirl of activity since dawn. It seemed an increasingly impossible task to feed, serve, dress and launder such a throng.

But at some point that afternoon, a miracle had occurred. They found the silver had been polished and dining table laid, the wine was already up from the cellar, the potatoes peeled, fowls plucked and cherries pitted. Nobody seemed to know when these tasks had been done or who was responsible for them.

'I could swear. . .' said Mrs Palfrey to Mrs Robinson, frowning at the potatoes and shaking her head. 'I *swear*. . .'

Mr Grey glanced up from where he was inspecting the household accounts. 'I took the liberty of arranging for a few small chores to be done while you were engaged elsewhere.'

Mrs Robinson was taken aback. 'That's, er, very kind of you. But I don't quite under—'

'Did I not assure you that the household would be amply served? You will find your duties become lighter, too, as the party progresses.'

Pattern and Nate exchanged looks. Stewards were

far too grand to go about peeling potatoes or polishing spoons, but who else could have done it? And how was it possible that nobody had witnessed the work being done? The other servants too were as puzzled as they were relieved. But since there was still plenty to be arranged, and precious little time to do it in, they were not inclined to fret over the issue.

Pattern wondered what Lady Hawk's guests were making of it all. She did not expect much from their servants – the Lane sisters' maid was as empty-headed as she was amiable, and neither Lord Charnly's loutish valet nor the Dowager's dowdy maid struck her as particularly enquiring types. (They had certainly paid scant attention to Mr Perks's speech on Sharing the Load, each claiming to be far too busy attending to their master or mistress to assist with other chores.) But the ladies and gentlemen were supposedly educated people. Surely *they* must be puzzled by the island's oddities.

Pattern, as a lowly third housemaid, had been assigned to attend to Miss Smith's needs. As a poor relation, entirely dependent on Honoria and Frederick

Blunt's charity, Miss Smith was little better than a servant herself. Taking her a wash jug before dinner, Pattern found her sitting by the window, staring out despondently over the service yard, an open letter on her lap. Having seen the other young ladies flit about, scented and silken, with costly jewels about their person, Pattern could not help feeling sorry for Miss Smith. Most of her luggage consisted of books, and she had nothing in the way of jewellery. She might have almost been pretty, had there been a bit of colour in her cheeks, and had her hair not been fixed so carelessly.

Miss Smith accepted Pattern's offer to dress her hair ('My older sister is a lady's maid, miss, and she has taught me something of the Art'), though she showed little interest in her efforts. Pattern's offer was not a selfless one, of course: she knew ladies were apt to gossip with their maids, given time and the right kind of encouragement.

'How are you liking Cull, miss?' she asked as she set about with the comb and pins. 'Very pretty, isn't it?'

'Yes,' the girl said broodingly. 'I suppose it is.'

She smoothed down her letter again: it was written in a vigorous hand, and worn and creased in a way that suggested it had been read many times. The blotches on it had the look of tearstains, Pattern thought.

'And so warm for the season!' she burbled on. 'It is an almost magical spot, I should think.'

'The gentlemen are certainly spellbound.'

Pattern detected a touch of bitterness in her tone. 'Miss Hawk has admirers wherever she goes.'

'And yet nobody knew anything of her until this season. She appeared as if from nowhere and – pouf! One flash of her eyes, and even the stoniest of hearts has melted.'

'I hope her success has not left other young ladies disappointed.'

'If so, the fault is not Miss Hawk's. It is a gentleman's responsibility to keep his word and behave in an honourable fashion. Of course, not all gentlemen are as honest or loyal as they appear. Quite the contrary, in fact –' Miss Smith stopped and bit her lip, flushing.

Poor lady, thought Pattern. It seemed very likely

that Miss Smith had once enjoyed a romance with one of the gentlemen present, probably the person who had written her the letter, and most likely Mr Ladlaw.

Miss Smith was surely right to describe the gentlemen as spellbound. But who had cast the spell? Cassandra Hawk, or her mama?

Chapter Six

~~ ⚬⚬ ~~

You must be guarded against the allurements of pleasure.
S. & S. Adams, *The Complete Servant*

~~ ⚬⚬ ~~

Pattern took a wrong turn on leaving Miss Smith and found herself in a shadowy warren of unused rooms with no furnishings, save a few bits of marble statuary and the trace of frescoes on the walls. Hearing voices a little ahead of her, she paused in the doorway of a small antechamber.

It was Lady Hawk in conference with Mr Grey.

'. . . any impertinent questions?' the mistress was asking.

'The servants are inclined to gossip, as servants do,' the old man replied. 'Thus far, it seems harmless enough. Of the ladies and gentlemen, there has been nothing out of the common way, though naturally the ladies are more inclined to suspicion.'

'Then I think we shall have a little musical entertainment tonight.'

'Very good, my lady.'

Lady Hawk's skirts swished past Pattern's hiding place. Pattern held her breath and kept very still. She did not know what this scrap of conversation meant, but she had a feeling it spelled trouble.

At the bottom of the back stairs, Pattern found she had just missed a scene of high drama. Jane, the housemaid, whirled past in one direction, and William, the footman, stamped off in another. The sound of cross words and slammed doors hung in the air.

'Whatever was all that about?' she asked Nate, who

had been keeping watch from the boot room.

'Lovers' tiff.' He grinned mischievously. 'Seems our gallant Captain Vain's set the cat among the pigeons.'

It was Alfred who had thought of the nickname 'Captain Vain', after noticing how the gentleman was drawn to any mirror he passed. Moreover, Captain Vyne's compliments to Jane, which seemed given out of habit rather than made with serious intent, were quite enough to cause upset between her and William.

Nate bent to pick up a small posy, which Jane had evidently thrown on the floor in disgust. Pattern drew nearer.

'Goodness, are those snowdrops? From the forbidden glade?'

'Poor William picked them to prove his devotion. Said he wasn't afraid of no snakes, nor no sneaking snake of a gentleman. Then Jane said honest men don't need to wrestle snakes; they just need to keep their promises. Whatever that means.' He thrust the posy at Pattern. 'Here. You take 'em. Didn't you say snowdrops was a favourite of yours?'

Surprised and touched, Pattern buried her nose into the blooms. They were ice-white, almost uncannily perfect, with a rich velvety scent. 'Thank you, Nate.'

He winked at her, tucked a stray snowdrop jauntily above his ear, and returned to the boots.

Pattern planned to put the posy in her room, but Mr Perks was on the warpath, and Mrs Robinson in a pother, so she tucked them in her pocket and returned to her duties. These included composing her first report for the Silver Service. It was to be in the guise of a letter to an imaginary sister, and while turning down the beds she set about drafting sentences in her head.

A previously agreed code would help with the task. That she 'was sorry to hear about the loss of Aunt Ethel's cat' meant that their suspicions were confirmed, and supernatural misdeeds were afoot. Mentioning that her knee gave her 'no trouble for the moment' signified that she was not in any immediate danger. The news that she had been 'unable to find any trace of Mother's hairpin' was in reference to Henry Whitby. Describing the wider situation was less easy, however,

and she struggled to communicate the strangeness of the island and her suspicions of Lady Hawk in suitably disguised terms. Part of her suspected this was, in any case, a pointless exercise. Mr Grey had told the servants that he would pass letters to the boatman who brought supplies from the mainland, but Pattern had little faith in this offer. If mischief was afoot on the island, Lady Hawk would not want it communicated to the wider world, and Mr Grey was clearly *very* loyal. Any correspondence might well be tossed into the sea.

While Pattern and her fellow housemaids were making the bedrooms ready for the night, the rest of the servants were seeing to the gentry's dinner. Their own food would not be served until nine o'clock, and Pattern had been feeling hollow with hunger for most of the afternoon. The others had managed to eat some of the leftovers from tea, but Pattern had been doing chores for Miss Jenks and missed her chance. In her effort to ingratiate herself with the lady's maid, she had offered to take Lady Hawk's pug on its daily walk, whereupon Miss Jenks immediately thrust the yapping creature into her arms, and instructed her to give it a bath and clip its nails while she was about it. Pattern had not received as much as a thank you for her pains, let alone any useful gossip.

So when the message came that all the servants were invited to listen to Lady Hawk play the harp to her guests, Pattern could not suppress a sigh of annoyance. It would delay the meal yet further, and eat into the precious ten minutes or so before bed that she was permitted to take as leisure. How was she to write her report now?

Since the evening was so warm, the party had eaten out on the terrace. Pattern had heard the laughter and the chink of cutlery as she had gone about her work upstairs. It had been no small task to move the dining table outside, and it meant an even longer journey from the kitchens for the footmen laden with steaming dishes. From the open doorway, she saw that the table had only been partly cleared, still littered with stained and crumpled linens, and the wilting garlands that had adorned the feast. Warm

air blowing into the house brought with it the scent of sea salt and jasmine, roses and earth.

The footmen had carried the harp from the music room and placed in the hall. It was a huge gilded thing, worked all over with carvings of blooms and birds, and Lady Hawk looked very regal as she took her seat beside it, dressed in purple satin, with her shining black hair piled high.

The ladies, wearing expressions of happy anticipation, and the gentlemen, suppressing yawns after sampling the wines at dinner, were seated in chairs before the harp. The servants, with throbbing backs and aching legs, arranged themselves on the stairs. Only Mr Grey was aloof, observing the scene from the door of the dining room. Pattern was reminded of how he and Lady Hawk had consulted earlier about the 'musical entertainment', and felt newly uneasy.

Lady Hawk swept her hand across the strings, and the harp shimmered into life. The melody was a very beautiful one, and Pattern soon forgot her aches and complaints. After a while, the lady began to sing. Her voice was low but very sweet. The lyrics were in some foreign tongue, and the rippling melody was full of both promise and yearning.

Pattern was absorbed by what she heard, yet she began to realize that the rest of the audience was more enthralled still. Servants and guests alike had glazed eyes, vacant smiles and altogether empty expressions. Only Mr Grey looked just the same as he ever did. And one other – Nate. He craned round to look up at Pattern, and rolled his eyes.

When the last strains of music died away, for a long moment nobody moved. Even when the applause began, everyone clapped with a dreamy slowness. Their faces remained strangely blank.

Lady Hawk rose to her feet and lifted up her arms. 'The night is warm; the moon is full. It is time to celebrate the first night of our revelries. Let us embrace this isle and each other – let us dance!'

Now Pattern knew for certain that magic was in the air, because the servants moved down the stairs to mingle freely with the guests, and no one batted an

eyelid. The Dowager ambled outside hand in hand with Mr Perks; Mabel the kitchen maid was asked to dance by Lord Charnly. Everywhere Pattern looked were similarly strange pairings.

'This is a rum do, make no mistake,' Nate muttered in her ear. 'Best keep our heads down and play along.'

Pattern did not need any further encouragement. She knew instinctively, as Nate did, that they must disguise the fact they were not under the same enchantment as everyone else. So she tried to look as if she too had milk-pudding for brains and, arm in arm with Nate, followed the rest of the party as they streamed out on to the lawn.

Mr Grey took out a fiddle and began to play a jig. It sounded like a sea shanty. A full moon – swollen and apricot – hung in the indigo sky. Light blazed from every window of the villa where there had been no lights before. As the music soared, the dancers changed their partners, back and forth and round about. Sometimes it was the fiddle that played, and sometimes the harp.

And whether the tunes were as wild as a storm or as gentle as moonlight, the dancers twirled with the same dreamy expressions, and the same empty eyes.

CHAPTER SEVEN

❦❦ ❦❦

Men frequently become the dupes of artifice.

Mrs Taylor, *Practical Hints to Young Females*

❦❦ ❦❦

Servants and masters parted at midnight after an hour of dancing, and everyone repaired to their chambers in the same dazed manner in which they had gambolled on the lawn. The music's power was miraculous indeed, for the gentry even managed the irksome business of making ready for bed without the help of their servants. Pattern thought she would never sleep, with so many wild notions capering around her head, but, in the event, sheer exhaustion overwhelmed her.

In the morning, no trace of the revelries remained. The table on the terrace had been cleared, the washing-up done and the kitchen restored to rights. Even the usual work proved lighter than expected, for the weather was so warm that the maids were spared the task of laying fires in the bedrooms, and the air was so pure – without any of London's smuts and soot – that household dusting was much reduced.

However, not every load had lightened. The chamber pots were still to be emptied into the slop bucket, and their contents taken to the privy. This was Pattern's least favourite duty, but as she dealt with the various swills and stinks, she reflected that it was perhaps not a bad thing to be brought so sharply back to earth.

Nobody made mention of the strange events of last night. 'It was very kind of the mistress to let us hear her music-making,' Mrs Palfrey remarked to the kitchen maids. This sort of acknowledgement was as far as it went. Today, nobody questioned who had cleaned up last night's dinner, or remarked on the unseasonal

weather, or even seemed particularly surprised when a fox was found lounging on the drawing-room sofa.

'Another of Lady Hawk's pets,' Mr Perks observed, quite unruffled. It was as if he could see no difference between the fox and the pug dog.

Pattern was anxious to talk to Nate. This did not mean she intended to ask for his help – the task of uncovering Lady Hawk's secrets was hers alone. In any case, she was not at liberty to speak of the Silver Service or Sir Whitby to anyone. But she was exceedingly curious to know what he made of last night's events, hardly knowing what to think of them herself. Although her Silver Service training had impressed upon her that sorcery came in all sorts of disguises, a topsy-turvy dance was not exactly the kind of danger she had prepared for. Yet magic was at work here – she was sure of it. Why else was her skin prickling hot and cold with strange dread?

She found Nate in the silver room polishing knives and humming one of Mr Grey's sea shanties.

'There you are!' he exclaimed. 'Here's a fine mess,

for everyone is bewitched except us two! I'd wager it's partly the air of the place, but mostly the sound of Lady Hawk's harp.'

His forthright manner surprised Pattern. When she first encountered the sinister powers at work in Elffinberg, she had taken refuge in common sense, making every effort to explain them away by rational means. By contrast, Nate seemed to have accepted the situation with remarkable ease.

'It is very shocking, don't you think? I can scarcely believe it,' said Pattern.

'Well, it could be that I'm mad, and everything I saw last night was a fever dream. But I trust my own eyes, and I trust my own brain. I trust yours too. And you agree with me, don't you?'

Pattern gave a cautious nod.

'The world's a stranger place than most folks like to believe. My pa used to tell me stories about the island he came from – oh, they was fearsome enough to turn a man's spine to jelly! He had a tale of a witch who sheds her skin and flies about by night in the shape of cat.

She sucks a person's breath out of them while they're sleeping. And there was a devil woman too, all dressed in gold with a cow's hoof instead of a foot. Pa swore blind he'd seen her himself one night, waiting under a cotton tree . . . ' A smile crept across Nate's face. 'Mind you, a bit of witchery seems a small price to pay for the sight of Mr Perks waltzing with the Dowager. When I saw him this morning, just thinking of it was enough to give me the fits!' His expression turned serious. 'So. Got any ideas as to why the two of us didn't go cuckoo?'

Pattern was a little unsure how to proceed. It was a great relief to find someone as sensible of the situation as she was. Yet how much could she trust him? She worried that if she took Nate into her confidence and told him of her investigation he might try to take it over. In the eyes of the world, after all, she was only a girl, and so the natural subordinate in any alliance. She wanted to retain the advantage of her insider knowledge. On the other hand, there was no doubt that Nate's quick wits would prove useful . . .

'Well,' she said, 'we can start by trying to pinpoint

what we did or didn't do that was different to everyone else. For example, did you have anything to eat from the tea?'

'Some hope! Mabel promised to save me one of them raspberry iced buns, but Alfred took it off me.'

'Interesting. I didn't eat any of it either.'

'You reckon there was some kind of sorcery in the cucumber sandwiches?' His face fell. 'What'll we do? We can't not *eat*.'

'No indeed. But the other possibility is the snowdrops bestow some kind of protection.' After Pattern's dealings with herbal remedies, she had a healthy respect for the power of plants. 'I was carrying the posy you gave me in my pocket last night, and I noticed you still had a piece of the flower clinging in your hair.'

Nate rubbed his hands over his springy dark crop. 'It ain't there now. But you might be on to something. It would explain all them deathly warnings about snakes, and how no good will come of going to that glade.'

'Either way,' said Pattern, 'it was the playing of the harp, and Miss Hawk's singing, that did the real

mischief. And that can be easily remedied – look.' She held out a set of earplugs, which she had fashioned from beeswax polish and a melted-down candlestick. 'If you like,' she said hesitantly, 'I could make you a pair too. Then if we are invited to hear the music-making again we have only to block our ears.'

'Hm.' Nate was considering her thoughtfully. 'Sharp as a box of knives, ain't you? It's almost like you've been up against this kind of hocus-pocus before.'

'Whatever do you mean?'

'Only that most girls would be having hysterics at the idea of being stuck on an island run by a witch.'

'Most girls are not as feeble as you suppose.'

'Well, *I've* got the heebie-jeebies, make no mistake.' He struck a comically heroic pose. 'But I'm working monstrously hard to hide it.'

Pattern was impatient to get to work. Last night's moonlit jig was doubtless only the start of Lady Hawk's sorcery, and she had a strong suspicion that Cull and the mysterious Italian island where Henry Whitby had disappeared were one and the same. A travelling island that floated across oceans . . . was it possible?

But suspicions were not enough – she needed evidence. Her efforts to draw information on Lady Hawk from Miss Jenks had met with no success. The lady's maid considered herself far too grand to associate with a mere third housemaid. In fact, she kept herself apart from all the servants, including the upper ones, insisting on having her meals in her own room. She refused to handle anything Nate had touched because she thought his dark skin was 'dirty', causing all the servants to dislike her even more. If only disloyalty to her mistress could be added to her faults! But she was too discreet about Lady Hawk to be of any use to Pattern.

Fortunately, the afternoon provided Pattern with her first opportunity to explore beyond the villa. The young ladies and gentlemen were also eager to see the sights, and so Lady Hawk directed the kitchen to make up hampers of food for a picnic. The party would go on a tour of Cull's scenic spots while their luncheon was

prepared. The two footmen and Mr Perks would wait on the picnickers, with assistance from Pattern. Since the other servants preferred to take their ease back in the villa, with only Lady Hawk and the Dowager to wait on, she met with no competition for the job.

Alfred and William were to go ahead to the picnic spot on foot, while Pattern would ride on the donkey cart with Mr Perks to transport the hampers, icebox and other fitments. Arriving at the stable yard with a bundle of rugs to begin loading the cart, she expected to see James, the coachman, or Jacob, the groom, but was instead met by the sight of Lord Charnly and his valet, Mr Stokes. His lordship had tired of inspecting the horses and was now tormenting a couple of cats.

His victims were the grey tom that lived in the stables, and the kitchen's marmalade mouser. Lord Charnly had tied their tails together with a bit of twine. The desperate creatures were scrabbling and clawing at each other in their frantic bid to get free, mewling piteously. Meanwhile, his lordship – normally so sour-faced – was chuckling heartily. His valet cheered him on from the side.

As the cats yowled and spat, Pattern could hold back no longer. 'Sir! Please – for pity's sake –' She rushed forward and, braving the slashing claws of the cats, endeavoured to uncoil the twine. Once freed, the animals streaked away as fast as their legs could carry them. 'For shame,' she said under her breath, as she sucked her scratched and bloodied hands.

Lord Charnly had heard her. He looked as amazed as if one of the heaps of horse dung on the cobbles had risen up and spoken to him.

But it was his valet who answered on his behalf. 'Hold your tongue, girl. It's not just feral cats that could do with a kicking.'

'The little maid's in the right.' Mr Grey had suddenly appeared in the yard. 'You should know by now that my lady has a passion for animals. She cannot abide cruelty to them of any kind.'

Lord Charnly curled his lip. 'Well, *I* cannot abide insolence from the lower orders. Your lady may run a

liberal household, but it seems to me her good nature is being taken advantage of. Both of you would do well to remember your place.'

'Vicious young brute,' muttered Mr Grey, as soon as master and valet had swaggered back to the villa.

Pattern ventured a timid smile. 'It must be very peaceful here as a rule. I am sure you rather dread the arrival of so many visitors.'

'Humph. It's nothing I'm not used to.'

'Oh? I thought Lady Hawk did most of her entertaining abroad. I should have loved to have served her last house party, the one on the Italian estate—'

'Italy?' he said sharply. 'Where did you hear that?'

'I *think* it was Italy they said.' Pattern was all innocent confusion. 'The other servants, you see, were talking about milady's travels. But it might have been France they meant. Or Switzerland . . .'

The old man's eyebrows bristled. 'Perhaps if you spent more time on your work and less on idle gossip, then your memory would improve.'

*

Pattern did not take Mr Grey's rebuke to heart. She was no longer the kind of girl to be cowed by the disapproval of her superiors. And, whatever dangers and difficulties might await her, she could not help but feel a skip of happiness as she and Mr Perks set off from the house. The sun on her face and breeze in her hair were the promise of freedom.

Cull's resemblance to an English landscape was decreasing rapidly. They drove along an avenue of slim, dark cypress trees, through an olive grove whose silvery leaves shimmered like the scales of a fish, past thickets of myrtle and orchards of lemon trees. The chirp of cicadas buzzed alongside the sigh of the sea. Although the island was less than three miles long, the dusty white road was so winding, and the hills so undulating, it felt as if they were traversing a much larger terrain.

Their destination was a summer house on the island's southernmost tip. It was in the design of a classical temple, with a domed roof and white marble columns. A golden statue of a nymph stood on the central pedestal, looking out over the sea to the faint

outline of the Cornish coast. At least, Pattern *thought* she glimpsed the mainland, but when she looked again mist had once more obscured it from view.

The sea was perfectly calm, its blue just one shade darker than the sky. Pattern lingered a moment to admire it and saw a large dark mass under the water, perhaps quarter of a mile away from the rocks below. She remembered the darkness beneath the sea she had noticed on the boat trip to the island. This shadow was also moving; not fast, but enough to leave foamy ripples in its wake. A whale, perhaps? But she could not stay to puzzle it out – she had too much to do.

It was hot work lugging the hampers into the summer house. Just because the meal was a picnic, the niceties of formal dining could not be abandoned. China, silver and linens must all be laid out on folding tables, and there was nothing particularly rustic about the menu, either. Pattern helped with the setting out of whole lobsters, roast duck, salmon, dressed salad, fruit tarts, jellies, custard, strawberries and cream, cheese, lemonade . . . not to mention copious amounts of champagne. She was still plumping cushions and shaking out the rugs when the party arrived.

James the coachman drove Miss Hawk, Adele Lane, Lord Charnly and Mr Ladlaw in the barouche. Captain Vyne drove the other carriage containing Alicia Lane, Miss Smith, Miss Blunt and her brother, the Reverend. As they disembarked, all exclaimed over the loveliness of the views and declared that the sea air had given them a marvellous appetite. The platters of food were cleared with quite remarkable speed, and the champagne consumption was not far behind.

While the party was feasting, the haze from the sea began to creep up the hill. Nobody remarked on it, which made Pattern nervous. She touched the posy of snowdrops in her pocket for reassurance. She was increasingly sure of their magical properties, for any ordinary bloom would have died by now – it had been two days. Although the snowdrops' strangely rich scent was nearly gone, and their heads drooped, they were still fresh white and green.

'There is a meadow of wildflowers just a little way

from here,' Miss Hawk announced, once the party had finished their meal, and were lolling on the cushions. Until this point, she had scarcely uttered a word except 'yes' or 'no' or 'very well, thank you' in response to her suitors' tender enquiries. 'I am sure Mama would be delighted if we were to gather some posies to take back to the house.'

Her guests needed no further persuasion. As one, they got to their feet and dusted off their clothes. Moments later, they were following her lead in single file down from the hill. Pattern was now on high alert – all the more so when she saw how quickly the party was swallowed up by the mist. Meanwhile, the servants got on with clearing the debris from the picnic.

'Mr Perks, one of the young ladies has left her parasol behind. Please may I take it to her?'

'Yes, yes, very good,' the butler replied, with the surprising vagueness that had lately descended on him.

By the time Pattern had reached the foot of the hill, the mist had thinned sufficiently for her to see the coachman snoozing in the shade of a tree, with the horses cropping the grass nearby. The rest of the party had dispersed in several different directions. A little way ahead, she found the ladies – save for Miss Hawk – silently gathering flowers. The mechanical, repetitive way they went about the task struck Pattern as highly unnatural, but since they did not appear to be in any immediate danger, she pressed on in search of the gentlemen.

The mist had begun to swirl around most confusingly, but she finally spotted the figure of Mr Ladlaw striding along the ridge over the bay. At least the haze provided cover for her pursuit, and after following Mr Ladlaw for only a short while, his path crossed with that of the Reverend Blunt, who was hurrying in the opposite direction.

After exchanging curt greetings, Mr Ladlaw indicated that he must not delay. 'I think it only fair to disclose that I am on my way to an assignation with Miss Hawk. She has invited me to view a particularly inspiring vista. She tells me it is most poetical.'

'Pardon me,' the other gentleman replied, 'but I fear

you must be mistaken. For I am on the way to meet with the lady myself, as there is a rare species of seabird she especially wishes to show me. She knows I am a keen ornithologist, and holds my knowledge of birds in high esteem.'

Mr Ladlaw gave the tolerant smile of a man given to humouring the insane. 'Well, well. It will not do to keep your feathered friends waiting. I bid you good day, sir.' He swept an ironical bow.

The Reverend returned it. 'Indeed,' he said coldly, 'I would not wish to disturb your flights of fantasy. Good day to you too.'

With that, they went their separate ways, both shaking their heads at the other's foolishness. And, indeed, Pattern could understand their confusion, because she was fairly certain she saw not one but *two* women in the mist. Each possessed the gleaming fair hair and slight figure of Miss Hawk. Each receded into the haze the nearer her suitor approached. Furthermore, they were not the only versions of Miss Hawk to be seen on the island – when Pattern looked behind her through the mist, she thought she glimpsed two more again in the vicinity of Lord Charnly and Captain Vyne.

Like the clergyman and the poet, each gentleman laboured under the delusion that Miss Hawk was waiting for them only a little way ahead.

'Miss Hawk! One moment – I beg –' wheedled the Captain, who had never had to chase after a girl in his life, and was not enjoying the novelty. Accustomed to being the handsome prince of any party, he had lost some of his natural advantage now that his hair was stuck to his forehead with sweat, and his eyes were set in a watery squint against the sun.

'Fair lady! I implore you to wait!' wheezed Lord Charnly, as he attempted to thrash past a thorn bush. Used to getting his way through bullying or brute force, the effort of appearing deferential was almost as much of a strain as his struggle through the undergrowth.

Pattern, perhaps because of the snowdrops in her pocket, was able to navigate far better than Miss Hawk's admirers. Even so, the mist had rendered the geography of the island so higgledy-piggledy and unpredictable

that it took her quite some time to find her way back to the summer house. In the meantime, the haze would momentarily part to reveal a sandy bay or stand of pine or grassy dell, through which the gentlemen blundered back and forth in increasingly frantic haste. And, all the while, the four Miss Hawks glided ahead of them, always just out of reach.

CHAPTER EIGHT

∽◌ ∽◌

For human savages, like other wild beasts, are allured by their appetites to their destruction.

Mrs Taylor, *Practical Hints to Young Females*

∽◌ ∽◌

It was a bad-tempered party that returned to the villa. The ladies had grass-stained skirts and, unaccountably, baskets of weeds and thistles in place of the wildflowers they had so painstakingly gathered. The gentlemen had sunburned noses and aching heads. Supper was by all accounts a most subdued affair, and Lady Hawk's announcement that she would play the harp again before

bedtime was not met with any great enthusiasm. This time, the ladies' and gentlemen's smiles of appreciation looked as strained as the servants'.

Pattern had not had a chance to talk to Nate since their conference that morning, but he tugged his ear at her before taking his place on the stairs, which reassured her that he had remembered to wear the plugs. Once everyone was in place, and more or less quiet, she carefully slipped the wax into position.

As soon as the music began, all fidgets and sighs ceased. Pattern could dimly hear the melody, but it was so muffled by the wax she would have felt reasonably safe from its charms even if she had not been in possession of the snowdrops. Once more, Lady Hawk's song was as mysterious as it was beautiful. Once more, everyone's faces were rapt with concentration, but emptied of any discernible real emotion or thought.

Pattern tensed when the music finished. Would they be expected to dance again? She was tired and footsore, and in no mood to pretend to frolic delightedly by the light of the moon. So she was relieved, as well as surprised, at Lady Hawk's closing words: 'You are weary, all of you. Sea air can be tiring when you are not used to it. Sleep well, dear friends, and soundly.'

All around her, Pattern saw people blink and stretch and look about. The vexations of the day had been smoothed away; as the servants prepared to attend to their masters and mistresses, it seemed to all intents and purposes an ordinary end to an ordinary evening. Pattern, however, sensed there was more to come. There was a tension in the air that made her skin shiver all over in expectation.

Then she saw Lady Hawk slip into the courtyard and go over to the cage of songbirds. She opened the gilded door, took out a chirruping finch and released it into the night.

Pattern had no idea what this meant, but it was sure to signify *something*. So although her own duties were over, and she herself should be going to bed, she lingered in the servants' hall. She was not alone: Mrs Robinson was inspecting some tablecloths, and Nate had just returned from his round of collecting boots, ready for cleaning in the morning.

Shortly before they were preparing to retire, the bell for Lord Charnly's room began to ring, violently. Mr Stokes the valet muttered an oath. He had his sights set on a cup of tea and his own bed. But back up he must go.

After only a short interlude, Mr Stokes returned.

'His lordship can't sleep. Says there's a bird squawking outside the window disturbing his rest. Nothing I can see or hear, but he's convinced of it.'

After conferring with Mrs Robinson, it was agreed they should move Lord Charnly to a spare bedroom in another wing of the villa. Pattern, as the only housemaid still up, went to make the room ready with Mrs Robinson's assistance.

While they were smoothing down the coverlet over the bed, Lord Charnly stamped in, resplendent in a dressing gown of scarlet silk, an ugly scowl on his face. Pattern reflected that the only time she had seen him truly cheerful was on the occasion he'd tormented the cats. Mr Stokes followed with his master's luggage, assisted by Nate. Pattern and Mrs Robinson curtseyed, but he swept past them to the window without a glance.

'Well, this is no use, is it? Either the damn bird's followed me here, or else there's a whole flock of 'em.'

'I am very sorry, milord,' said Mrs Robinson, 'but . . . I confess I cannot hear anything.'

'Then your ears are as deficient as your wits.' He flung open the shutters with a crash. 'There! Can't you see? It's hovering *right outside*. Fluttering and squawking and tapping its devilish beak against the masonry. Tap, tap, tap! Squawk, squawk, squawk!'

The servants exchanged looks. There was no bird to be seen or heard. The night outside the window was dark and silent, utterly serene.

Mrs Robinson tried again. 'Perhaps, milord, we could move you to another bedroom. I regret that it will not be quite as comfortable, but—'

'Enough. There is obviously a plague of these pests upon the house. Fortunately, I know how to put a stop to them. Hey, you –' this was to Nate – 'fetch me my fowling piece.'

When Nate wavered, the man bared his teeth in a snarl. 'Good God, do I need to fire shots up your backside? Jump to it!'

Nate jumped to it. He ran to the gun room to fetch the fowling piece while Mr Stokes helped his master get back into his breeches and boots. From outside in the hall, Pattern and Mrs Robinson could hear Lord Charnly's curses and complaints. It was a wonder the rest of the household was not raised from its beds, but a heavy slumber lay upon the place. Finally, Lord Charnly crashed open the door, snatched the shotgun from Nate's hand and waved everyone back with an angry gesture. 'You have already proved yourselves worse than useless. Out of my way, all of you.'

'Get along to bed,' Mrs Robinson told the others wearily, as soon as his lordship had stamped away down the hall. 'There's nothing more we can do. The gentleman has made it clear he wishes to be left to his own devices.'

Without exchanging a word, Pattern and Nate made for the back stairs, but instead of parting ways at the turning to the sleeping quarters, they hastened outside to the service yard. Here Pattern came to a halt.

'Nate, wait – you need to take some of these snowdrops.' By now, the flowers were wilting sadly, but rot had not yet set in. 'They are unlikely to protect us from bullets, but it may be they have other defensive powers.'

Nate nodded. His face was set, but his eyes were bright. It was plain he knew as well as she that a phantom bird was very likely only the beginning of the night's marvels. The air fizzed with dangerous possibility.

The sky was clear, so it was easy to make out Lord Charnly on the lawn, silk dressing gown billowing over his boots as he stalked back and forth, muttering oaths

and shaking his fist at the heavens. Now and again he took aim with his weapon, though no shots had yet been fired. The villa loomed behind him, dark and silent, without any sign of life.

It was not long before Lord Charnly's invisible prey drew him to the terrace at the end of lawn, and from there down into the formal garden below. The pebble paths and marble statuary glowed white in the moonlight. Pattern and Nate followed, taking cover behind a large piece of topiary hedge. At first Lord Charnly was so preoccupied with his invisible tormenter he did not notice he was being trailed. But then Nate's tread caused a twig to snap underfoot, and the man pounced.

'Oho, what's this? A couple of dirty brats come to play hide-and-seek!'

With the gun tucked under his arm, he seized each by the ear and dragged them out into the moonlight.

'We're very sorry, sir.' Nate tried not to squirm under the man's pincer-like grip. 'We only followed you in case – ow! – in case there might be anything your lordship needed.'

'How excessively helpful of you. Well, seeing as you're here, I'd best put you to use, then.' Lord Charnly let go of their throbbing ears, but his smile was not a pleasant one. 'You, boy – stand over there, by the cedar tree.' And, when Nate hesitated, he fired the shotgun into the air, causing both children to cower. Lord Charnly laughed delightedly at the sight. He seemed to have forgotten all about the invisible bird now he had human quarry. Pattern, indeed, wondered if he might be possessed: there was a mad glint in his eye that she had not seen before.

'That's right, boy: back against the tree – tall and straight now. And you, missy – go fetch an orange or one of those lemons to put on your friend's head. Now's as good a time as any for some target practice, don't you think?'

Pattern's heart was hammering fit to burst. The fowling piece did not fire single bullets but a spray of shot; Nate was likely to be very badly wounded, if not

outright killed. What use were magical snowdrops now? They offered no protection from a maniac shooting in the dark.

Nate looked very unhappy indeed, but he did as he was told and stood with his back against the cedar. Pattern pretended to go and look for fallen fruit among the moonlit paths, trying desperately to think of an escape plan in the meantime. So far, the best she could come up with was to dash a flower pot against his lordship's head.

'Stop dawdling,' the man called out. 'I can see an orange tree right over there, by that urn. That's right, quick as you can . . . *Now* what's the matter? Look alive, girl. You are goggle-eyed as a dead fish!'

Pattern was indeed frozen in shock. She was staring at two of the statues behind his lordship. They had begun to stir.

The first to move was a goddess wearing a crescent-moon headdress, with a quiver of arrows on her shoulder and a bow in her hand. She shook out her hair and wriggled her shoulders, as if waking from a refreshing nap. Then the figure of a centaur – a creature with the upper body of a man, and the lower body of a horse – pawed the ground with a stony hoof. The goddess raised her bow, and plucked its invisible string. Nate had seen what was happening too, and let out a yelp.

Lord Charnly turned at the noise. Pattern saw the instant his first flash of disbelief turned to naked terror. Still, he didn't lack courage – she would grant him that. He aimed his gun, only slightly unsteadily, and shot the marble woman straight in the face. The shots bounced off the stone harmlessly.

There was a moment's pause. Then he gave a strangled sort of cry and turned and fled.

He was stumbling out of the garden towards the olive groves. The two living statues did not immediately move after him, but surveyed the scene in a leisurely fashion. The goddess took a step towards where Nate was standing under the cedar. Jolted out of his stupor, he at once began to clamber up into the shelter of its branches. 'Penny, *run!*'

Even as Pattern started to move towards the villa,

the centaur was upon her, and scooped her up in his stony arms. As effortlessly as if she had been made of paper, he lifted her above his head and placed her on his back – the back of a horse, whose flesh and muscle and blood and bone were all solid marble. Then he put the horn slung across his chest to his lips, and blew three sharp, piercing cries.

The goddess lifted her arms. Her voice was like a cold wind blowing off a mountainside. 'Let the wild hunt begin!'

The lawn in front of the villa began to bubble.

The bubbles spread. Turf swelled and heaved. Formless lumps were hauling themselves out of the ground, twisting themselves into new shapes. The shapes solidified as grass and mud took on the texture of fur and the weight of flesh and bone. Animals were pulling themselves out of the ground and shaking the last scatters of earth from their ears: big cats, wolves and wild boar, and domestic beasts too. Pattern was sure she could see the donkey from the orchard, as well as the grey cat from the stables, and the marmalade one from the kitchen.

But even the domestic animals looked far from tame. Moonlight gleamed on teeth and fangs and claws, and the reflected glow of so many pairs of black and golden eyes had a reddish tinge. The night vibrated to the sound of snarls and growls and snapping jaws, rising to yelps and howls as the menagerie sniffed the air for the scent of their quarry.

Where was Nate? Pattern could see no sign of him against the darkness of the tree. She dared not try to jump down from her mount, for she would fall straight into the jaws of the beasts that surged about below. She did not know if the centaur had put her on his back to protect her from the pack, or whether he had some other sinister plan in mind, but it seemed as if she was going to be carried off by the hunt regardless. She twisted and turned on her stony steed, and tried to fight a rising tide of panic.

At another blast from the centaur's horn, the motley pack surged forward, and the two statues followed. The goddess ran ahead, stone feet striking against the

pebble-strewn ground. The centaur followed at a trot, though Pattern still had to clutch at his carved upper body to keep her balance. The sudden chill that had taken hold of her did not help matters. It was making her feel oddly stiff, particularly in the legs.

'Psst! Penny! Up here!'

She looked up. Nate had shimmied on his belly along one of the tree's lower branches: the one that stretched over the path to the olive grove. As the centaur passed under the tree, Nate reached down to grab Pattern under the arms, lifting her off the statue's back.

It was no easy task. The strange heaviness in her legs was dragging her down, and Nate grunted and grimaced under the strain of her weight. Fortunately, he did not have to hold her for long. Even if the centaur had noticed the loss of his rider, he did not stop or turn, but increased his pace from a trot to a gallop, as the goddess raced alongside.

Only a few moments after the last of the hunt left the garden, Nate was forced to relinquish his grip. Dropping heavily on to the ground beneath the tree,

Pattern found herself bruised and shaken, but otherwise unharmed.

'I owe you a deal of thanks,' she said, with only the merest tremor in her voice, as soon as Nate had scrambled down the tree to join her.

'What's happened there?'

He was pointing at her feet. The soles of her shoes gleamed white in the moonlight. How heavy they felt! Her toes, too, were cold as ice. Pattern let out a gasp.

'Oh heavens – I – I think . . . I think my shoes have turned to *stone*.'

'Quick, let's get 'em off you.'

Her hands were too much of atremble for her to untie the laces on her own, so Nate had to help. It took all Pattern's self-control not to let out a sob with relief when she found her toes were just as they should be, although oddly chilly to the touch. For, sure enough, the soles of her shoes were solid marble.

'We got you off that horse-man-creature just in time,' Nate said. 'A few minutes more, and who's to say your feet wouldn't have turned to stone along with your

shoelaces? And I suppose the rest of you would have followed soon after . . .'

Relieved as she was at her escape, Pattern could not help but feel dismayed at the loss of her shoes. She only had the one pair. 'Whatever am I to do? I can hardly spend the rest of our stay in my stockings.'

'I got an idea.' Nate pulled out the wilting snowdrops from his pocket. 'Here goes nothing,' he said as he rubbed the flowers energetically against the stone. 'Ha! Look at that. I ain't London's best bootboy for nothing.' Sure enough, the sap from the flowers had restored Pattern's shoes to leather.

'Well,' she said, 'the snowdrops may not have been much defence against bullets or magic beasts, but they have come to my rescue all the same.'

'Speaking of bullets . . . what's become of his lordship?'

With all the excitement, they had nearly forgotten about him. They got up from the grass and hurried to the edge of the garden. In the light of the moon, they could see that the hunt was already spreading out from the olive groves and into the hills, where the distant speck of Lord Charnly could just be seen, running for his life.

'Those creatures look just as likely to tear him to pieces as turn him to stone,' Nate said. His voice shook.

Pattern nodded. She did not trust herself to speak. The blue skies and warm scents of Cull had charmed her, in spite of herself, so that moonlit jigs and the phantom Miss Hawk had appeared as little more than magical mischief-making. Now she saw the evil of the island for what it was.

CHAPTER NINE

Quarrels are much more easily avoided than made up.

S. & S. Adams, *The Complete Servant*

Nobody remarked upon Lord Charnly's disappearance the following morning. It was as if he had never been with them at all. His belongings had vanished, and there was no sign of his valet either.

There was, however, a new addition to the statue garden. Down among the pebble paths and topiary hedges, the nymphs and other mythical creatures had been joined by a very different figure. It was the carving of a man in a dressing gown, his face twisted in terror, as two monstrously fanged cats sank their teeth into his booted heel. By the look of it, the statue had been there for some time, patched with moss and stained by the weather. The toe of the right boot was somewhat chipped.

'What a curious ornament!' remarked the Dowager Duchess, as she strolled among the roses with Miss Blunt and Miss Smith after breakfast.

'It is certainly a fine example of the sculptor's art,' replied Miss Blunt. 'Yes,' said Miss Smith. 'The man's features are excessively lifelike. One might almost suppose he is ready to speak – or, rather, scream.'

Pattern overheard this exchange because she was the other side of the hedge, on her way to harvest more snowdrops. The sight of Lord Charnly's statue made her shudder. She would never forget the icy feeling in her toes, nor the numbing stiffness in her limbs, as the stone began to creep up her body. Unfortunately, it was too late for his lordship. Although a handful of snowdrops had been enough to save her shoes, releasing

the gentleman from his marble prison would likely require a whole glade of flowers.

She still intended to equip herself and Nate with as many of the blooms as she could manage. The flowers had already come to her aid in unexpected ways. Who knew what other miracles they might perform?

Her other plan had been to cut the strings of Lady Hawk's harp, since it was the evening concerts that kept people so dazed and docile. But when Pattern had crept into the music room with her sewing scissors, she found the instrument was locked away in a painted case. In any event, even if the harp was broken, Lady Hawk could still sing and, for all Pattern knew, it was her voice rather than the harp's music that did the mischief.

For now, the snowdrops were her best defence. Pattern would have liked to think that Mr Grey's warnings of snakes were simply to scare people away, but she had heard William boast to Alfred of his heroics in picking the posy for Jane. He swore that he had beaten off 'a great black-and-yellow serpent' with a gardening rake. Alfred had laughed, shaking his head.

Pattern, however, was inclined to take the story more seriously. Accordingly, she had armed herself with a toasting fork and a poisonous concoction of cleaning products. She had spent a great deal of time perfecting the recipe, and was rather looking forward to testing its effects.

However, she had only got as far as the gate at the end of the garden, when Mr Grey appeared. 'And where might you be off to, missy?' He was eying her basket with suspicion.

'Well, my, ahem, throat has been rather sore, so I was going to pick some blackberry leaves to brew a tea. I heard there was a bramble bush by the wood . . .'

'There are no brambles on this island. It is very unusual to fall ill here, for the air is remarkably healthful.'

'None the less, sir,' she said, as firmly as she dared, 'my throat *does* hurt.'

'Doubtless a consequence of excessive gossiping.' His frown was a fearsome sight. 'Never mind the blackberry leaves. You would do better to drink hot water with honey and lemon – and refrain from tittle-tattle.'

'Thank you, sir. I will be sure to try that.'

He didn't move. 'Then you will find everything you require in the kitchens.'

Frustrated, Pattern had no choice but to make her way back to the house, Mr Grey following close behind. She found the servants' hall in uproar.

'Oh, Penny! What do you think,' Elsie gabbled, 'but Reverend Blunt has just insulted Mr Ladlaw, who has called him out in a duel!'

'Great heavens! How can that be?'

'Well, it began this morning when Mr Ladlaw read out a poem in praise of Miss Hawk's eyes. The Reverend said its sentiments put him in mind of a Sunday School tract. Then Mr Ladlaw said the tedium of the Reverend's sermons was enough to convert any Christian to devilry. So the Reverend—'

'But how are they to fight? Is it to be pistols at dawn?'

'No, they are to fence out on the lawn, and milady says that everyone may watch!'

Pattern hastened to join the servants clustering by the door and at the ground-floor windows. By wiggling to the front, she had a clear view of the 'field of honour'. Captain Vyne was to be Mr Ladlaw's second, and Mr Grey acted as the Reverend's. It would be their responsibility to supervise the encounter.

For weapons, the gentlemen had taken the rapiers that had been mounted over the fireplace in the smoking room. They were both frowning as they paced about, practising thrusts. Neither had the look of natural athletes. The poet had a slight build and bony wrists, whereas his adversary, the priest, had the lumpen physique of a man far too fond of second helpings at dinner-time. Captain Vyne – who was nearly as expert a swordsman as he was a seducer – surveyed them both with a highly superior air.

The ladies were arranged on the terrace. Iced lemonade and bowls of bon-bons were on hand for their refreshment. They were all threatening to swoon at any moment, though none of them would really be so foolish as to miss any of the excitement for the sake of a faint. Pattern found it disturbing that neither the Reverend's sister, Honoria, nor Mr Ladlaw's former

sweetheart Miss Smith seemed particularly distressed.

'I do hope Frederick puts on a decent show,' said Miss Blunt. 'He was never much of a sportsman at school.'

'There is something very splendid,' mused Miss Smith, 'about the gleam of sunlight on a finely honed blade.'

'Aren't they *dashing*?' cooed the Lane sisters, as the Dowager nodded and smiled.

Meanwhile, Miss Hawk – the subject of the duel – and her mama looked entirely unmoved. Miss Hawk was petting the little pug. Lady Hawk was placidly setting out cards for a game of patience.

After the Seconds had ensured the duellists were in position, Mr Grey held a white handkerchief aloft. After a heart-stopping pause, he dropped it to signify the fighting was to begin.

A delicate and deadly dance began. The two men circled each other warily, now and again making feints and thrusts. When all of a sudden the blades clashed in earnest – *snicker-snack!* – the ladies gasped, and even

Pattern felt a not unpleasant thrill.

With renewed speed, the duellists darted and dashed hither and thither. Steel swished through the air, meeting with a quiver and a clang. Reverend Blunt scored the first hit, scraping the point of his blade down Mr Ladlaw's arm. A thin line of red scribbled through the poet's white sleeve.

The audience broke into applause. One of the footmen whooped; the ladies cooed admiringly. Pattern hoped that the drawing of the first blood would signify the end of the duel, but it seemed the fight had only just begun.

'It is . . . it is not to the death, is it?' she asked Alfred.

He did not take his eyes off the match. 'Who cares? I've never seen such good sport. It's a deal more exciting than cock-fighting, anyways.'

Nobody seemed particularly alarmed. As for Miss Hawk, she might as well have been observing a game of bridge.

Now it was Mr Ladlaw's turn to score. His blade slashed through the Reverend's waistcoat, causing him

to stumble and curse. However, he recovered almost instantly. Despite their physical differences, the pair were remarkably evenly matched.

Pattern was no expert, but as time wore on she was sure that there were at least two occasions when either gentlemen could have scored a disabling, if not fatal, hit. Instead, they contrived to scratch flesh or tear cloth without inflicting any serious damage. Pattern should have been relieved by this. Nobody would wish for a man to throw his life away so recklessly. Yet she did not think the duellers were deliberately holding back. Indeed, they were straining every fibre of their beings in the effort to land a killer blow. Their eyes bulged with frustration; their teeth gnashed with fury.

Dart forward, dance back.

Twist, lunge, thrust, parry.

Whisk, whisk! Snicker-snack!

Both gentlemen were sweating and panting with effort. Torn breeches flapped, sleeves were slashed, buttons sliced off and stockings shredded. Each were spotted and speckled with blood from nicks and scrapes. How much longer could they continue before one or other of them dropped to the ground from sheer exhaustion?

The ladies continued to accompany the action with tremulous oohs and ahhs and smatterings of applause. Miss Hawk popped another sugared bon-bon into her mouth, and Lady Hawk quietly attended to her game of cards. Pattern watched her turn cards over and move them about for some moments before she noticed it was a very odd version of patience, if that was indeed the game. For Lady Hawk appeared to be arranging the cards according to colour, rather than suit. It struck her that the way the red and black cards were placed might be related to the progress of the duel.

She shifted her position so she had a better view of the spread. Pattern watched Lady Hawk delicately place an ace of diamonds face down on the table, and the very next moment Mr Ladlaw cried out as the Reverend Blunt's blade scraped his ribs. A little while along, it was a knight of clubs that was turned over, and Mr Ladlaw who scored a hit. The longer Pattern

watched, the more she was convinced that the red hearts and diamonds represented the poet, while the black clubs and spades represented the clergyman.

Nate had clearly come to a similar conclusion. He worked his way round to Pattern's side and, under cover of the general applause, muttered: 'Like watching Punch and Judy, ain't it? No prizes for guessing who's the puppet-master.'

'Or mistress, rather,' Pattern said grimly. She picked up a jug of lemonade that William, its original server, had left on the steps. 'I think I can put a stop to it, but I need some way of stumbling that does not look contrived.'

Nate held out a piece of bon-bon to Lady Hawk's pug, which was snuffling for treats along the terrace. 'Leave it to me.'

Pattern carried the jug to where the ladies were seated, on the pretence of refreshing the Dowager's glass. When she drew near to where Lady Hawk was sitting, Nate threw a piece of the sweetmeat towards Pattern's feet. The greedy pug immediately scrambled after the treat, and under her skirts. Pattern let out a little shriek.

She had meant to 'accidentally' slop lemonade on to Lady Hawk's card game, but her intervention was more dramatic than she intended. The pug was so startled by Pattern's yelp that it leaped into Lady Hawk's lap and from there to the table. As the creature snuffled and scrabbled, the playing cards flew every which way about. The lady exclaimed angrily in a foreign tongue.

'I am s-so s-sorry, milady!' Pattern was a picture of mortification. 'The dog – it came from nowhere – forgive me—'

Miss Jenks was already springing into action, and scolded Pattern soundly. Lady Hawk brushed dog slobber from her skirts, a look of intense displeasure on her face – but not suspicion, Pattern was relieved to see. She was even more relieved that the two duellists had abruptly ceased their fight and were sitting on the lawn, slumped over their blades, and panting.

'I think,' drawled Captain Vyne, 'that we had best declare it a draw.'

CHAPTER TEN

Avoid as much as possible being alone with the opposite sex.

S. & S. Adams, *The Complete Servant*

That evening before supper, Alfred saw Miss Hawk slip a note into Captain Vyne's hand. He reported this to William, who shared it with Jane, who passed on the news to her fellow housemaids. While the others girls were exceedingly interested and impressed by this development, it made Pattern very anxious indeed. If Miss Hawk was arranging an assignation with the Captain, it was sure to end badly for him, particularly after what she'd witnessed with Lord Charnly.

Pattern did not know what was coming, or what she could do about it, but the strange prickling energy she had sensed last night was once more in the air. Earlier in the day, Mrs Palfrey had discovered a rainbow-coloured parrot in the pantry, and a leopard napping in the library had given the Dowager a start, yet nobody seemed in the least bit concerned by the wild beasts and birds making themselves at home in the house. Nor had any of the servants enquired as to the whereabouts of Lord Charnly and his valet, Stokes. Whatever magic was at work, its power was only increasing.

When, after supper, the gentlemen joined the ladies in the drawing room, the Captain took the first chance to slip away. Pattern followed. He was heading to a small study at the end of the hall. It was one of those rooms that put Pattern in mind of Nate's observation that the house was dressed like a stage set, for, in contrast to the austere Classical style of most of the

villa, this cosy book-lined den would not look out of place in a country vicarage. Miss Hawk's sewing basket rested on one of the leather armchairs.

Pattern hesitated at the door. She could think of no good reason for being there, but the Captain seemed pleased to see her. 'Aha. Fetch me a light, would you? It's damnably dark.'

The only illumination came from the moon shining through the window. Pattern would have thought the darkness contributed to the air of mystery that surrounds romantic assignations. However, when she hastened back with a candle, she saw what the Captain had in mind. There was a full-length mirror along one of the walls, in which the gentleman wished to inspect his reflection.

'That's right. Bring the light here.' He smoothed down his hair, turning this way and that to see his handsome profile at its best advantage. It was little wonder he had such a bewitching effect upon the ladies. 'Higher, if you please.' He was peering at the glass, trying to make out a tiny imperfection above his eyebrow. 'Damn midges . . .'

As the candlelight brightened the glass, the mirror began to shimmer. It sparkled and swirled, a pool of quicksilver. Alarmed, Pattern took a step back. As she did so, the glass swung forward off the wall. The mirror was, in fact, a hinged door.

'Good Lord,' said the Captain, squinting at the shadowy interior it had revealed. 'A hidden passageway! How quaint.'

'It is probably not safe, sir. In these old houses, such structures are often unstable.'

'Nonsense.' He poked his head into the darkness. A ripple of laughter could be heard from within. 'By Jove, that's Miss Hawk! Sounds like she's just around the corner.'

'Please, sir, I really don't see how she can be. Sir, I beg you to reconsider. I fear – I fear a trap of some kind. I do not think you are aware of the danger—'

'Fear? Danger? Ha! An officer of the Royal Dragoons is not afraid of a bit of dust and spiders! Give me your candle. Quickly, now . . . Don't look

so downcast, little mouse. Faint hearts never win fair ladies, y'know!'

With a wink and a smirk, which were no doubt intended to be dashing, he stepped jauntily into the narrow opening, pulling the mirror door shut behind him. Pattern sprang after him, only just in time to prevent it closing. She had a strong feeling that once it did, it would not open again. She propped it open with *A Naturalist's Guide to Cull* pulled from the bookshelves and hurried over to Miss Hawk's sewing basket—

'What's going on?'

Pattern started, but it was only Nate; he had clearly followed after her. In different circumstances, she might have been annoyed at being shadowed, but she was relieved to see him. She gave him the story as quickly as possible.

'I am going after the Captain, but I will leave the end of this piece of embroidery silk tied to the leg of the sofa, and take the rest of the skein with me. If I tug on the thread, then you are to fetch help – and if you tug on it, I will come back straight away.'

'You can't go there alone! It's sure to be a trap of some kind. Who knows what manner of monster could be lurking in there?'

'Nonetheless I must go,' she said firmly as she lit a fresh candle. Nate was not employed by the Silver Service; he should not endanger himself for Captain Vyne's sake. 'I cannot explain why, but you have to trust me when I say I have . . . well, I have a special obligation to stop Lady Hawk's schemes.'

Nate looked ready to protest further, but there was no time for debate. 'Please, I beg you to stay here and watch the thread, and ensure the door stays open for our return.'

He was frowning. 'And if one of the other servants or a guest should find me here?'

'You'll think of something – I'm sure of it. See you soon,' she said, with more confidence than she felt, as she slipped through the mirrored door.

It was very dark inside, in spite of the candle Pattern carried and the chink of light from the gap in the door.

The walls and floor of the passage were made of rough-hewn stone. But only a little way ahead, the passage made a sharp left turn, and the darkness suddenly burst into light and life.

Pattern was surrounded by endless images of herself, above, below and to either side of her. She was in a corridor made entirely of mirrors. She spun round, and the reflected Patterns spun round too; identical startled frowns on their identical faces.

Even though the space was not particularly narrow, she immediately felt breathless, cramped. There was no escape from herself: even the ground was a mirror, in which countless more Patterns were multiplied into space. It seemed she had moved beyond the physical confines of the villa into some other dimension. The bounce of candlelight between the mirrors dazzled her eyes, increasing her disorientation. She clutched at her little coil of silk thread and took a deep, steadying breath. After walking only a short way, she reached a crossroads.

'Captain Vyne?' she called out, and her voice echoed hollowly. She thought she heard an answering shout. It seemed to come from her left, and so she turned that way. As she rounded the corner, the corridor split into four, sending multiple reflections cascading in yet more directions. It was like being in the centre of a kaleidoscope.

'C-Captain?'

'Here!'

The sound came, very faintly, from the second of the four branching corridors. At least she *thought* so; the echoes made it hard to be sure. And the next turning was even more disorientating, for in this corridor the wall of glass was subtly curved so that the mirrors' reflections were distorted further.

Pattern had heard of such tricks at fairgrounds, where she could see that it might be amusing to view oneself monstrously stretched or squeezed. Here, it was nightmarish. She squeezed her eyes shut and shuffled forward, making her way by touch alone, running her fingertips along the cool, smooth glass.

'Captain Vyne . . . are you there?'

Another shout, which sounded like a muffled curse, echoed eerily from somewhere ahead. Pattern approached another crossroads.

As she continued unspooling the thread behind her, she regretted not keeping better track of her progress. She seemed to remember there was a trick to navigating mazes – weren't you supposed to keep your hand on the wall at all times? Or always turn to the left? Something like that . . .

Another faint shout, or curse, or cry, came from somewhere ahead.

'Stay where you are! I'm coming to find you!'

Then she felt the thread twitch.

Someone was pulling at it. *Nate*, she thought, and her heart clenched. Was he in trouble? Had they been found out by Lady Hawk? Or was it a trap, to lure her back out of the maze before she could help the Captain?

The thread of silk was tugged again, with new urgency. The moment of decision was agonizing. But she could not risk Nate being in trouble, especially after he had saved her from the centaur. Then there was the danger of the thread breaking, in which case both she and the Captain would be trapped.

'I'm sorry!' she shouted helplessly into the kaleidoscope of glass. 'I have to go. But I'll come back . . .'

She retraced her brief journey through the maze, feeling more breathless and dizzy with every step. Her

foreboding was justified, for when she finally tumbled out of the door, she found Nate with Miss Hawk's hands wrapped round his throat.

'You should not be in this room,' Miss Hawk told him, and it was in the same mild, quiet tones in which she was wont to remark on the weather. Her unblinking blue eyes were fixed on Nate's face. As Pattern watched, aghast, she lifted him up with her tiny hands, so he dangled helplessly in her grip, legs thrashing, a good three feet above the floor.

'Let him go!' Pattern cried.

Miss Hawk turned and regarded her calmly. 'You should not be here either. Presently, I will punish you too.'

Still holding Nate round the neck, she glided to the mirror door and kicked it shut. Pattern was unable to stop her: the young woman's strength was superhuman. As Pattern had feared, once the door was closed, it instantly sealed itself against the wall. There was no way back into the maze – and no way out for Captain Vyne.

Right now, however, Pattern had other problems

with which to contend. Miss Hawk had begun to squeeze Nate's neck. Flailing wildly, he tried to scratch at her face as he choked and gasped. Pattern tugged and kicked, but she might as well have been attacking a figure made of marble. There was not so much as a scratch on Miss Hawk's smooth flesh. The only damage Pattern could inflict was to her clothes as, with a ripping sound, three of the tiny pearl buttons on the back of her gown popped off.

Pattern stopped her attack. She was transfixed at the sight the gaping dress had exposed: a small metal enclosure between Miss Hawk's shoulder blades. It was similar in size as well as appearance to the winding hole on a clock. Whether or not the girl was Lady Hawk's real daughter, Pattern had always supposed her to be under some kind of spell. A horrible idea struck her – what if Miss Hawk was not flesh and blood at all? What if she really *was* the living doll she so closely resembled?

But mechanical things could be broken. As Nate's face grew purple, and his splutters yet more desperate, Pattern rushed to fetch the brass key belonging to the

clock on the mantelpiece and jammed it into the metal hole in Miss Hawk's back. She turned it counter-clockwise as forcefully as she could. A creaking sound came from somewhere deep within Miss Hawk, like the squeaking of rusty gears. She released Nate so abruptly, he fell to the floor in a heap. Afterwards, she kept to her place, swaying slightly and blinking rapidly, turning her face this way and that.

'Wh-wh-what *is* she?' Nate asked hoarsely, once he had recovered sufficiently to speak. He sounded like his throat was red-raw and bruised.

'An automaton, I think.' Pattern spoke more calmly than she felt. She needed to set a professional example, after all.

'A whaty-what?'

'A kind of self-operating machine. Like a wind-up doll or a clock.'

'Then that must be the key to the contraption.' Nate pointed to the girl's neck, and the little gold charm in the shape of a key she always wore. It was much smaller and more delicate than the key Pattern had wedged in her back, and was inset with tiny diamonds. 'Hey now – if we take the key, does that mean she'll wind down and stop working sooner or later? That'll put a spanner in Lady Hawk's plans.'

This was an excellent idea, and Pattern felt a prick of annoyance that she had not thought of it herself. 'I am sure Lady Hawk will keep a spare key somewhere. But it is a start.' Pattern undid the clasp of the necklace and put the little key in her pocket. She glanced at the clock and was surprised to see their misadventures had only taken twenty minutes. 'Poor Captain Vyne! I fear he is lost to us.'

'What happened behind the mirror?'

Pattern briefly described the maze, and Nate explained his own misadventure.

'Miss Hawk, as soon as she saw the open door, went to close it, and when I tried to stop her, that's when she turned on me. Her eyes flashed with this cold blue light. And her hands! Like being grabbed by iron pincers, it was. Even so, I'm right sorry for having to pull the thread.'

Pattern was sorry too, but she could hardly hold it against him. 'We have made real progress,' she assured him. 'Disabling Miss Hawk may well be the first step on our way to rescuing her suitors. But now we must set things to rights and get out of here before her mama or anyone else comes looking for her.'

They spent several minutes tidying the study and removing all evidence of their tussle. The doll continued to jerk and twitch, but did not move from her position and was otherwise passive. She put up no resistance as Pattern tidied her hair and straightened her dress, even managing to quickly re-sew the tiny buttons on the back of her gown using the threads in Miss Hawk's sewing basket. However, Pattern was fearful about what would happen once she removed the key. Would the doll go into spasms and break down completely? Or would she move to attack them again?

Nate was armed with a brass candlestick in case they needed further defence. Yet once her mechanics were un-jammed, the Miss Hawk doll merely smiled at them. 'I must go back to my mama,' she murmured.

'Is everything well, miss?' Pattern asked hesitantly.

'Quite well, thank you.'

'Were you, er, looking for something?'

'I was going to meet the Captain. I see he is not here. That is as it should be.' She glided to the door. 'Goodnight.'

Pattern and Nate exchanged glances. The doll clearly had no memory of what had just taken place. There was no visible damage except that her head was tilted ever so slightly to the left, and there was a faint, very faint, clicking sound as she walked. But even if Lady Hawk did not notice these signs of injury, she would be sure to miss the charm from round her so-called daughter's neck. It would not be long before she realized that someone was working against her.

CHAPTER ELEVEN

It is impossible for a dishonest person to be a good servant.

S. & S. Adams, *The Complete Servant*

They may have fought off an automaton, but Nate and Pattern's work was not finished for the night.

'Nate, Penny, what d'you think you are doing, idling in the hallway in plain sight? Penny, I would have expected better from you. From both of you, in fact. Get back to your work!'

It was Mr Perks, with an expression of severe displeasure. With mumbled apologies, Nate and Pattern were forced to go their separate ways. Pattern's took her past the drawing room. As Alfred went through the door with a fresh pot of coffee, she could hear both Miss Hawk and her mama among the voices within.

Soon the evening's music-making would begin; Pattern had very little time to act. If Lady Hawk kept a spare key to operate her doll daughter, then it was most likely in her bedroom. Pausing before its threshold, Pattern felt almost more nervous than when she had stepped into the mirror maze. Her next actions would amount to a declaration of war when found out.

The room was very tidy, which was a relief, as it meant Miss Jenks had already turned it down and would not be up again until it was time to get her mistress ready for bed. The only sound was the thumping of Pattern's heart. Her blood seemed to be filled with pins and needles. After a moment's indecision, she went to the ivory jewellery box on the dressing table. But, glancing at the mirror there, she had a dreadful shock, as Captain Vyne's face suddenly appeared like a ghost behind the glass. He wore a very anguished expression.

Pattern blinked, and the image vanished, to be replaced with her own frightened reflection.

With renewed determination, Pattern opened Lady Hawk's jewellery box. The treasures inside were dazzling: ropes of diamonds and pearls, brooches crusted with crystals and earrings dripping with gems. If the key was the same as the one that Miss Hawk had round

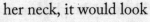

her neck, it would look oddly plain among these extravagant baubles. Pattern moved to the bedside table and opened the drawer. It contained some monogrammed

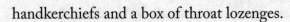

handkerchiefs and a box of throat lozenges.

Did witches suffer from sore throats?

She rattled the lozenges. Nestled among them was a small gold and diamond key.

'*What* do you think you are doing?'

It was not Lady Hawk, but it was almost as bad: Miss Jenks.

She was standing in the doorway with a pile of petticoats, staring at Pattern and the open drawer. Pattern had started when Miss Jenks spoke; did she look as guilty as she felt? Pattern thanked her lucky stars she was not standing anywhere near the jewellery box, and that she had taken care to shut the lid.

Even so, she knew how suspicious the scene appeared. Any moment now, Miss Jenks could accuse her of theft and summon the authorities – starting with Mr Perks and Mrs Robinson, followed by Lady Hawk and ending with a magistrate. Many servants had been left to rot in the country's gaols as the penalty for pilfering from their employers. Although Pattern's predicament was not as grave as being lost in a maze of mirrors, or hunted by a pack of wild beasts, it was still trouble of a high order.

Pattern gave a timid smile and opened the palm of her hand to reveal the throat sweet she was holding. The key was tucked into the cuff of her sleeve.

'Please, I'm very sorry, but my throat has been painfully sore, and I thought taking just one of the sweets wouldn't do any harm.'

Miss Jenks's naturally haughty expression grew haughtier still. 'You thought rummaging through milady's personal effects, stealing her property, was *harmless*? No. *I* know where these things lead. It starts with the filching of a throat sweet and ends with grand larceny. Why are you in her private chamber, anyway?'

Pattern's thoughts raced as rapidly as her heart. 'I . . . I was returning this handkerchief –' she pointed to one of those inside the drawer – 'which I found dropped on the stairs. Since I was passing the room, I thought it easiest to return it myself.'

'You are the lowliest of the housemaids. You should leave the thinking to your superiors.'

'I'm very sorry.' Pattern hung her head. 'I did not mean to get above myself.' She twisted her hands. '*Please* don't get me into trouble. I'll make amends, I swear.'

Miss Jenks was enjoying herself. She made Pattern

wait before giving her answer. 'Very well. I have seen that you're good at needlework, so you can do all my mending for the rest of our stay, as well as giving that horrid little pug its daily bath and walk. Then – as long as you continue to be quiet and respectful and keep to your place – I will agree to say no more about it.'

'Thank you. Oh, thank you, Miss Jenks!'

'Now be off with you, before milady arrives.'

Pattern hurried away to find Nate in the boot room, feeling a little shaky at her narrow escape. She felt shakier still when she imagined how Lady Hawk might react when the time came to wind up Miss Hawk's mechanisms and no key could be found. Though she knew it was a weakness in a secret agent, she was in need of a kind word and a friendly face.

'Nate . . . what if Lady Hawk casts some kind of spell to find the keys?'

Pattern was fretting now.

'Then we'll just have to put them beyond use.' Nate produced a pair of pliers and the hammer used for small household repairs and set about bending and twisting

the gold out of shape. 'Don't worry – I've a good hiding place in mind.'

'Have you? Where? Are you *sure* you—'

'Leave it be,' he said, more sharply than she had heard him speak before. 'I said I'd deal with it.'

A booming musical note was heard: Mr Grey had taken to striking a gong when it was time for the house to gather to listen to Lady Hawk's harp. Bed would immediately follow, and Pattern had little choice but to go on her way. Besides, her head was too cloudy with tiredness to think straight. The sooner this day was over, the better.

But rest was in short supply that night. Pattern was woken in the early hours of the morning by the sound of slamming doors and raised voices.

'Out of bed, both of you, and stand in the hall,' cried Mrs Robinson, crashing into the room Pattern shared with Elsie. They had never seen her looking so stern, even though her hair was in curl-papers and eyes groggy with sleep.

'W-whatever's the m-matter?' Elsie stammered. 'Is it burglars? Or fire? Heavens! Is it *pirates*?'

'There's a thief in this house,' came the grim reply. 'Every servants' room is to be searched. Stay here and don't move an inch.'

All the female servants were lined up outside their rooms, shivering in their shifts. Pattern's heart hammered wildly in her chest. She was even more uncomfortable when she saw Lady Hawk herself, fully dressed but with flashing eyes and dishevelled hair, stalking the corridor.

'I want all the beds stripped and their mattresses overturned,' she commanded. In her agitation, her accent was stronger than usual. 'Every seam and stitch of clothing must be undone if necessary! Tear up the floorboards; tear down the walls! I will not rest until my property is found and the culprit punished.'

The way she spoke was blood-curdling.

What had Nate done with the keys? No doubt Mr Grey and Mr Perks were searching the menservants' bedrooms right this minute. Even though Pattern

knew quite well that the stolen property was not in her possession, she had an illogical fear that Lady Hawk would be able to sense her guilt. Indeed, she had played the part of faithful servant for so long that part of her *did* feel guilty. To steal from one's employer was the ultimate sin. She could not quite shake off the shame of her transgression.

Besides, there were items in her possession that might not bear up to close inspection. These included a spy-glass, a pair of steel knitting needles sharpened to knife-point and a cleaning spray that could fell a man at ten paces.

By the looks of it, she was not the only servant to feel exposed. Elsie had gone very pale. Jane was chewing her nails. Miss Jenks was trembling. Did they all have secrets to hide? Or was it just the frenzied nature of the search that alarmed them? Thumps, crashes and curses could be heard as Lady Hawk and Mrs Robinson began the hunt. So far, only Mabel and Ellen's room had been turned over, revealing nothing more incriminating than a dog-eared *Magazine of Marvel and Curiosity*. Then—

'Thief!' came a cry. 'Villain! Traitor!'

Lady Hawk surged out of Miss Jenks's room and cuffed her maid on either side of the head. Mrs Robinson followed after her. She was holding a handful of trinkets: silk ribbons, lace collars, a pearl hairpin and a sapphire ring. They were the kind of knick-knacks that a gathering of fine ladies might mislay without immediately noticing. Yet Lady Hawk cared for only two items, which she now thrust into Miss Jenks's face. It was too dark to see what she was holding, but Pattern knew what they were. A pair of little gold and diamond keys, bent out of shape.

'Wicked, shameless girl! Did you really think you could hide them from me?' Lady Hawk's eyes flashed. There were spots of colour high on her cheeks.

The maid was glassy-eyed with shock. 'I-I don't . . . I c-can't . . . I—'

'Lucky for you they were found so quickly, else I would have used my powers to flay the truth from your bones.'

Miss Jenks had begun to snivel and shake. 'But I

n-never saw them b-before . . . I did not take them . . . N-never ever . . . I swear it!'

'Liar!' Lady Hawk, always so serene and gracious, was an entirely different creature: one of fire and fury. 'You are not only a thief, but a vandal, for I see you have beaten the metal down to try to prise out the stones. You have *no idea* of the damage you've done . . .' She paused, eyes glittering feverishly. 'Or *have* you? What do you know? *Who is behind this?*' She took the maid by the shoulders and began to violently shake her.

Miss Jenks's mouth gaped. 'N-nobody,' she stammered. 'N-nothing. I know nothing, milady, I swear. I don't know how the keys got there. I – I don't know how any of these things got into my room. None of it! I am innocent! Someone is framing me! There must be another thief –'

Her eyes slid towards Pattern.

But then Jane stepped forward. She had spied something glinting in the heap of stolen trinkets Mrs Robinson had put on the floor, and outrage gave her voice. 'Why, that's my silver thimble, the one my grandmother gave me. I've been hunting high and low for it these past two days! And isn't that Mrs Palfrey's Sunday-best brooch?'

That decided the matter. 'So you not only rob your mistress and her friends,' said Lady Hawk, 'but you steal from your own fellows too.'

Miss Jenks continued to protest her innocence, but much more weakly. 'It is a plot, a lie, a terrible mistake . . .'

Lady Hawk curled her lip. 'Your guilt is written all over your face. It is plain to see what you are: a common, sneaking, lying thief. And, though you do not know it, the injury you have done me is far graver than mere robbery.' She turned to Mrs Robinson. 'Take her away and lock her in the coal-hole. First thing tomorrow, she leaves the island.'

CHAPTER TWELVE

◌◌ ◌◌

Our comfort requires us to be patient with other people . . .
you know not how you may irritate.

S. & S. Adams, *The Complete Servant*

◌◌ ◌◌

Miss Hawk came down for breakfast as usual, but her movements and speech had slowed, and there were very faint creaking noises from within her person. Although the two gentlemen were oblivious, the ladies noticed that something was amiss.

'Are you quite well?' Pattern heard the aged Dowager enquire, as she served tea to the ladies in the morning room. 'You seem a little out of sorts.'

'I am perfectly well, thank you,' Miss Hawk replied, though her eyebrows and fingers continued to twitch.

The Lane sisters exchanged arch looks, and Miss Blunt smirked into her sleeve. What a relief to find that even the perfect Miss Hawk had her flaws! Only Miss Smith's spirits did not seem raised by the discovery that Miss Hawk was not feeling her best. She was tucked in a corner with a book and engaging as little as possible with the conversation.

Lady Hawk, too, was unusually silent, pacing by the window, a preoccupied frown on her face. Even if she was satisfied that her maid was an ordinary thief, she was still faced with the problem of what to do once her 'daughter's' mechanisms ran down completely. Her eye fell on Miss Smith. 'What are you reading, my dear? That does not look as if it comes from my library.'

The book was, indeed, as old and shabby as the rest of Miss Smith's belongings. 'It is *Tales from Ovid*, my lady.'

'Ovid! I would have thought a dusty old poet

made for rather dull reading.'

'I have always found the Greek myths very interesting, my lady.'

'Then perhaps you would be so kind as to allow me to take a look?' But Lady Hawk did not give her much choice in the matter. To Miss Smith's bewilderment, and the other ladies' amusement, she plucked the volume out of Miss Smith's hands and tucked it under her arm, before striding out of the room.

Pattern found the confiscation of the book most intriguing, but, trapped as she was with the teapot, she was not in a position to see where Lady Hawk had taken it. Besides, she was anxious not to do anything that might attract her mistress's attention. The servants' hall talked of little else but the scandalous Miss Jenks, and it was assumed that Mr Grey had arranged for her to be taken away by boat at first light to be delivered to the local Cornish magistrate. Pattern hoped this was true, and that Lady Hawk had not found some more unusual punishment for her faithless servant.

As for handsome Captain Vyne, he had vanished

from people's memories as completely as the vicious Lord Charnly. Nobody else seemed to notice that every mirror in the villa contained a blurred and distant image of the Captain, screaming soundlessly, and banging his fists against the glass.

'However did you know Miss Jenks was a thief?' Pattern demanded at her first chance to speak to Nate in private. She had been itching to talk to him since breakfast, but somehow there were always other people in the way, or other tasks to be done. She found him washing down the passageway outside the pantry – one of the tame wolves that had taken up residence at the villa having left a pile of droppings there.

'I saw her pinch a coin from Lady Hawk's purse once,' Nate said, without looking up from the floor. 'And, back in London, she had these handkerchiefs that had somebody else's initials sewn on 'em. It weren't hard to find where she stashed her loot; I just peeked beneath the mattress and there it was. So I shoved the keys down under the other end, and figured that if

someone uncovered one lot of stolen property, they'd be bound to find the keys soon after.'

Pattern frowned. 'It was fortunate Lady Hawk did not inflict some terrible punishment on Miss Jenks, as she did with the two gentlemen. Framing her was a reckless move.'

Nate threw down his mop. 'Listen here: for all we know, Lady Hawk could've hunted down her keys with magic. Then if they'd turned up in any ordinary hiding place, she'd know for sure someone in her household was out to get her. This way, we've bought ourselves some time – time to put a stop to Lady Hawk, and protect *everyone* on this island. Yes, I'm sorry about Miss Jenks – for all that she were a nasty piece of work – but we didn't have a whole lot of choices, as I recall. So maybe you should get down from your high horse for a minute.'

'What do you mean?'

'I ain't forgotten what you said just before you went into that mirror maze. You hinted how you was part of something bigger, something secret, that you won't or can't tell me about. All right, then. But you can't ask for my help and order me about, then expect me just to shut my mouth and get on with it. We're *both* of us servants, remember.'

Pattern flushed. 'I have never ordered you about.'

'No? "Stay here, keep back, do this, do that, don't ask questions . . ."'

Pattern was ashamed. In Elffinberg, when she had joined the Grand Duchess Eleri's battle against her uncle, she had resented being bossed about and not listened to, when she knew her ideas were good ones. It was only when she began to stand up for herself that she and Eleri became true friends. Had her membership of the Silver Service gone to her head?

'I *want* to get stuck in,' Nate continued. 'Course I do. After all, it's in my own interest that we get off this devilish island in one piece, and not get turned into a pair of pumpkins or what have you. But that don't make me your skivvy.'

'You're right,' said Pattern, 'and I'm sorry.'

'You know, it ain't weakness to ask for help. It don't

make you any less clever or capable.'

Now Pattern felt a different kind of shame. Nate had been brave and loyal. He deserved better treatment from her, but his abilities were also a valuable resource. She had been in danger of letting her pride get in the way of her doing the best possible job.

She took a deep breath. 'I cannot reveal everything of my history, but I can say that I am here on behalf of the family of a young man who went missing while courting Miss Hawk. He too was invited to an island gathering where strange things were afoot. So, yes, I was prepared to encounter Dark Arts when I joined this household. That does not mean I feel at all confident in my efforts to repel them. I am very thankful to have your assistance.'

Her speech was more formal than she intended, and she spoke somewhat stiffly; perhaps this was why Nate did not look entirely satisfied.

'You really can't tell me who you're working for?'

'It is not my secret to tell. It's not that I don't trust you—'

'I'm glad to hear it,' he said, heatedly, 'seeing as how I saved you from being turned into a garden ornament.'

'And I am truly grateful, believe me. Not just for your help, but . . . but for your companionship also.'

Nate chewed at his lip. 'All right. I understand you got prior loyalties, or what have you. But whoever sent you to this island ain't here now. You got me, or nothing. So how about the two of us make a pledge of our own – a pledge to help each other, and trust each other, and work as a team. Agreed?'

'Agreed.'

Pattern solemnly shook his outstretched hand. It was heartening to know their alliance was now official, for it struck her with renewed force how lonely and uncomfortable her time on Cull would be if she did not have Nate to talk to.

'But don't think I've given up on winkling out your secrets,' he added. 'One of these days, I'm going to get the whole story out of you, Miss Penelope Pattern.'

*

Pattern and Nate's new alliance was soon put to the test, for their next challenge was to gather more snowdrops. Thanks to the shrinking of the house party, and the general absent-mindedness of those tasked with serving it, they were able to slip away without too much trouble. Even more fortunately, Mr Grey was locked in consultation with Lady Hawk, and so was not around to block their way to the forbidden glade.

'A snake is not the most fearsome creature in the world,' said Pattern. 'William beat it off with a rake. I believe reptiles are scared of fire too.'

'Ah, but you can catch more flies with honey than with vinegar,' said Nate.

'You think we should try to tame it?'

'Did you never see a snake charmer at a fair? There was an Indian fellow I saw once, with a great big turban and a beard, and a cobra in a basket. Now, the snake began to hiss and spit, but then the Indian, he played a tune on his pipe, and the creature calmed right down till it was docile as a baby. You'd swear it even had a grin on its face.'

'But I am not musical . . .'

'Don't matter.' Nate pulled out a penny whistle from his pocket. 'I am.'

The wood, when they reached it, was silent and cool, and the glade as starry with flowers as Pattern remembered. The trees were laced tightly overhead, blocking out nearly all the sun, and the velvety green scent of the flowers was almost overpowering. The scene looked entirely innocent. Pattern moved towards the nearest clump of snowdrops and tightened her grip on the trowel she had stolen from the garden shed.

At once, the flowers in the centre of the glade began to stir. Something was making its way through the undergrowth. In moments, a thick snake, its scales patterned in checks of black, brown and yellow, was pouring itself over the ground towards her. It gave a rasping hiss, revealing the red arched roof of its mouth and razor-sharp fangs.

Pattern jumped back and dropped the trowel on the ground. Her flesh crawled. However, once the creature saw that she had retreated from the flowers, it came no further,

flicking its forked tongue at her from its snowy bed.

Nate swallowed hard. Then he took out his penny whistle and moistened his lips. After a few false starts, he managed a wobbly version of 'Scarborough Fair'.

Pattern inched forward. The snake, which had been drawing its head back as if ready to strike, paused and flashed its amber eyes.

Nate tried again, this time performing 'The Bluebells of Scotland', with only three wrong notes. The snake put its head to one side, as if to listen more attentively. Nate moved on to 'Over the Hills and Far Away'.

'I think it prefers the Scottish melody,' Pattern

whispered. She had a strange notion that the markings on its back resembled tartan.

Nate kept tootling away, increasing in fluency as he increased in confidence. It was true the snake seemed to be much more soothed by the Scottish folk tunes. On hearing 'Auld Lang Syne', it even began to sway back and forth, as if in time to the music.

Nate launched into 'My Bonny Lies Over the Ocean'. Finally the snake's eyes drooped.

Heart in her mouth, Pattern darted forward with the trowel and thrust it as deeply as she was able into the rich black earth. She was lucky: the soil was loose, and a clump of flowers – roots and all – came free in just two vigorous scoops. Nate kept playing all the while. Once Pattern had wrapped the roots in a wet handkerchief and placed them in her basket, they were ready to go. Slowly and cautiously, still playing on the pipes, Nate backed away, Pattern at his side.

They planted the snowdrops in a neglected corner behind the servants' privy. With any luck, the plants

would grow here undisturbed, replenishing their supply. Pattern's sense of relief did not last long, for on returning to the villa she discovered what had really happened to Lord Charnly's valet and Lady Hawk's maid.

It was eleven o'clock and the grandfather clock in the hall was striking the hour. Pattern had never paid it any particular attention, but on this occasion she glanced up as she heard the chimes. As the bell was struck, little panels to either side of the clock face flew open, revealing two miniature figures. One was a man, the other a woman, both dressed in the dark clothes of upper servants. Small as the automatons were, their features were plainly recognizable as Mr Stokes and Miss Jenks. They leaped in and out of their hatches in time to the chimes of the clock, before being shut up completely as the last echo died away. Pattern shuddered at the sight.

For the first time, Pattern allowed herself to think what would become of them all if she – and Nate – failed to stop Lady Hawk. It was clear the enchantress's prime target was Miss Hawk's suitors. But what would become of the rest of the gathering once they were despatched? While the gentlemen were not entirely sympathetic characters, the ladies seemed harmless enough, and the remaining servants were honest and hardworking.

Pattern had been reassured by the fact that when Henry Whitby disappeared, everyone else who had attended the party returned home unharmed. She was no longer comforted by this thought. The fate of Mr Stokes and Miss Jenks suggested that, on this occasion, Lady Hawk had no intention of letting *anyone* off the island.

One of our most impressive recruits . . . Well, that could no longer be true. Pattern was perilously close to failure. So much for Mr Crichton's confidence in her, so much for Mrs Jervis's trust and Sir Whitby's hopes! She knew her enemy, and she could guess the fate of Sir Whitby's ward, yet could do nothing about either. Alas, she doubted any of her coded letters to the Silver Service had left the island. Cull was entirely

cut off from the outside world.

Instead of rescuing Henry Whitby, it looked as if Pattern was going to be in need of rescue herself.

Pattern could not afford to dwell on her troubles. Now that her and Nate's expedition to the woods was complete, she had to make up for lost time and devote herself to the duties of a housemaid rather than those of an investigator. She was preparing to dust the ground-floor reception rooms when she was distracted by the smell of burning. The smell drew her to the study where Captain Vyne had met his fate. It was the only room in the villa where the maids still laid a fire, as the Dowager liked to retire there for a nap after meals, and the old lady was liable to feel a chill even in Cull's warm air.

Pattern found someone had stuffed papers in the grate so forcibly that the fire was nearly choked out, and could only smoulder and smoke. She dug around in the hot ash with the tongs, and was most surprised to pluck out the charred remains of a book. With a jolt of excitement, she realized it must be the volume of

Greek myths that Lady Hawk had confiscated from Miss Smith. Why had Lady Hawk been so anxious to destroy it? What secrets might it reveal?

The pages were mostly burned away, although the singed spine and part of the contents page remained. The names of the tales were all entirely unfamiliar to Pattern, though she thought they might be arranged in pairs of names. Orpheus and Eurydice; Perseus and Andromeda; Glaucus and Scylla . . .

'What is the meaning of this?'

Glaucus Grey, the steward, was looming behind her.

CHAPTER THIRTEEN

❦

Even the remissness and ingratitude of our servants may furnish us with a lesson.

Mrs Taylor, *Practical Hints to Young Females*

❦

Pattern scrambled to her feet and attempted to dust ash off her hands. 'One of milady's books appears to have fallen into the fire, so I was attempting to recover it . . . Please, sir, but is this who you were named after?'

The steward's eyebrows shot upwards at her impertinence. 'I *beg* your pardon?'

Pattern showed him the sooty list of contents.

'Glaucus and Scy – Scy –' She stumbled over the unfamiliar word.

'It is pronounced *Silla*,' Mr Grey snapped. Then he gave a slightly self-conscious cough. 'But the similarity in wording is a coincidence only. Glaucus is an, er, old Cornish name.'

Pattern did not find this entirely convincing.

'Lady Hawk enjoys the art of the ancient world,' she said. 'This house is full of treasures from that time. I would have thought she liked the stories too.'

'My lady's reading habits are no business of yours. You are a housemaid, not a librarian.'

But Pattern pressed on. 'One can learn from books in quite unexpected ways. I used to think fairy tales were for children . . . till I met a man who said they contained many truths about the world.'

Mr Grey's face grew dark. 'The Greek myths are not fairy tales. There are no happy endings in them. There is only blood and madness and tragedy. Mortals suffer and are punished, while the gods laugh.'

A chill went down Pattern's spine. She began to

wonder anew about Lady Hawk's abilities, and how deeply rooted the woman was in the bloodstained powers of stories of the past. The island, she thought, had the feel of something ancient as well as foreign. But what was Mr Grey's place in all this? He appeared to be Lady Hawk's faithful servant, yet his words about the Greek myths felt more like a warning than a threat. Perhaps it was not affection for his mistress that kept him loyal, but fear.

'I find you interesting, young Penny,' the old man continued. 'Interesting . . . and curious. We have not had such an enquiring visitor for a very long time. I wonder if, despite all my warnings, you have been trespassing among the snowdrops again? I wonder if it is mere coincidence that my lady's projects have met with recent difficulty?'

She supposed he was referring to the mechanical failure of Miss Hawk. 'I am very sorry to hear milady is experiencing difficulties,' she said blandly. 'I had not noticed it.' Her heart was banging against her ribs, but she told herself that if the old man was going to turn her over to Lady Hawk then surely he would have already done so.

'Don't forget your place, little maid. Those who tangle with the powers that be are apt to get their fingers burned.'

Then he took the sooty remains of the book from her hand and poked it back into the grate, using the bellows to send the flames leaping upwards so that sparks flew, and the fire hissed.

Luncheon was taken out on the terrace, which allowed Pattern to observe the party from the windows of the adjacent rooms as she went about her work. First, however, she had to shoo away another of Lady Hawk's pets – a black-and-white-spotted pig that had made its home in the dining room. It grunted in a most aggrieved manner when Pattern closed the door on its snout.

By midday, Miss Hawk was twitching and creaking worse than ever, and although her voice often stammered to a stop, her powers of fascination still held the gentlemen. No matter how persistently

the other ladies enquired after Miss Hawk's health, or how many meaningful remarks they made about fragile constitutions and nervous disorders, the gentlemen resolutely failed to take the hint. The Reverend Blunt and Mr Ladlaw were tireless in their devotion. Despite their collection of bloody scrapes, no reference was made to their recent duel, and they were icily polite to each other at all times.

Thus far, Pattern had found Mr Ladlaw something of a puzzle. He was generally silent and brooding, and kept himself to himself when not attending to Miss Hawk. As part of her preparations for infiltrating the party, Pattern had read those of his poems that had appeared in the *London Poetical Review*. They had been melancholy musings on nature and its hostility to man, and, though Pattern did not really feel qualified to judge, it seemed clear he had talent. She had also taken the time to read his book, *The Towers of Callabrio*, which displayed the same descriptive powers as his poetry, but was considerably more entertaining, with a very strong-willed heroine, and full of romantic, supernatural and blood-curdling adventure.

It was exactly the kind of novel that female servants were strongly discouraged from reading. Indeed, Mrs Minchin, principal of the Academy of Domestic Servitude, had always said such books corrupted the mind and led to all manner of Moral Decay. Pattern, no stranger to blood-curdling adventure herself, still found herself turning the pages of *The Towers of Callabrio* with increasing interest and urgency. A little moral decay was a risk worth taking for such excitement, in her opinion.

However, Mr Ladlaw's talents had suffered a steep decline since coming to Cull. When tidying his room, Pattern had found the scribbled drafts of love poems to Miss Hawk. They were extremely dreary ramblings in which his beloved was described as possessing curls 'as golden as Cupid's bow', lips 'like two dancing cherries', and eyes that were 'pools to drown love in'. But perhaps it was unfair to judge them *too* harshly, given the man was labouring under an enchantment. Pattern was more interested in the fact that the handwriting was a match for the letter over which she had found Miss Smith

sighing. It had been a love letter, she was sure of it.

The Reverend Blunt was an easier man to get the measure of, and the more Pattern saw of him the more she disliked him. Over luncheon on the terrace, the conversation turned to Miss Jenks, for over the course of the morning the story of her crime had travelled through the house. Lady Hawk remained distracted and out of sorts, unwilling to fully engage in the conversation. Nonetheless, the ladies and gentlemen took up the subject enthusiastically, united in their outrage.

'Betrayal in servants is a very particular evil,' proclaimed Honoria Blunt. 'For at least your common criminal is not living in one's home and eating one's food, all at one's own expense.'

'I must confess that I never liked the look of Miss Jenks,' said the Dowager. 'She dressed far too finely for a servant.'

'Yes,' said Adele Grant, 'there was something sly about her, I always thought.'

'Perhaps it was the smallness of her eyes,' suggested Alicia.

Miss Smith, as was her custom, just drooped and sighed.

No one was more outraged than the Reverend, however. He was one of those Christians who believed forgiveness is God's business, and punishment man's.

'Of course the wretched woman should face the full weight of the law,' he began. 'Too many servants have grown soft and idle through good living, resulting in an altogether shocking sense of entitlement. It is this laughable sense of their own importance that leads them to abuse the trust of their betters. Such treacheries are a kind of modern plague.'

Pattern, busy rubbing linseed oil into a chair leg, heard all this through the open window overlooking the terrace. She thought of what the Silver Service had uncovered about the Reverend stealing from his own charity, and had to bite down on her lip. Miss Jenks, at least, had not defrauded poor widows and orphans.

'Alas,' the Reverend continued, 'I fear the country as a whole is entering a steep decline. I see evidence of this all the time as I go about my work in the

parish. Unwed mothers, feckless fathers, shirkers and layabouts! The trouble is that these people – the most vicious and unprincipled of the lower classes – do not *wish* to be saved. On the contrary: they revel in their depravity.' He took a hearty slurp of wine. 'But we can take comfort, as always, from the words of the Lord. For, as the Good Book says, "Evil shall slay the wicked: and they that hate the righteous shall be desolate."'

'Quite so,' said Lady Hawk. Her preoccupied mood had lifted; her voice had new energy. 'Dear Reverend, you are very kind to take such a keen interest in my servant troubles. I do hope you will accept Mr Grey's invitation to go on a boat excursion this afternoon. It is quite the best way to see our seabirds to their full advantage. The Cull cormorant is a treat not to be missed.'

So Reverend Blunt was next in line for punishment! And Mr Grey was somehow involved. Pattern reminded herself that even if the steward obeyed his lady's commands out of fear, he still remained loyal to her bidding. As she moved from oiling wood to polishing brass, she had to suppress a sigh at the thought of going into battle on Reverend Blunt's behalf. Not only was he a thief and a hypocrite, but, for such a young man, he really was *excessively* pompous . . .

Shortly after her mama's remark about the Cull cormorant, Miss Hawk announced that she was suffering from a headache, and would therefore retire to her room for the afternoon. Satisfied that his rival could make no gains in his absence, the Reverend was only too pleased to agree to Lady Hawk's plan for a bird-watching boat trip. Meanwhile, Mr Ladlaw offered to entertain the party by reading from his novel. Even the servants were invited to listen.

Pattern was relieved Mr Ladlaw was safe, at least for the moment. Sulky looks and bad romantic verse were hardly the same kind of wickedness as the Reverend's thievery, Lord Charnly's violence or the hearts broken by Captain Vyne. Indeed, she was starting to wonder if the gentlemen's time on the island was actually a process of elimination, a bizarre kind of contest with Miss Hawk as the prize. Did Lady Hawk mean to give

the poet Miss Hawk's hand in marriage as the reward for being the *least unpleasant* gentleman in the party? Not that Miss Hawk was any great trophy, of course. A wind-up doll rather than a flesh-and-blood woman, and a malfunctioning doll at that . . .

Pattern's final task in the drawing room was to wash down the paintwork. Moving from the skirting board, she paid particular attention to the windows and frames. This provided her with a good view of Miss Smith. While Cassandra Hawk's damage was mechanical, Miss Smith gave all the signs of someone who was suffering from an injury to the soul. She had become even more careless with her dress and hair, and her shadowed eyes and wan complexion suggested sleepless nights and anxious days. Pattern, returning to her theory that Miss Smith and Mr Ladlaw had once enjoyed a romantic understanding, felt another spike of bitterness towards Lady Hawk. It was all the more cruel to make a young man fall in love with an automaton when there was a real young lady to whom he had already promised his affections.

How much she had to discuss with Nate! While Pattern had been at the housework, he had promised to try to slip a snowdrop into the gentlemen's coat pockets as a precaution, since it was clear that both Mr Ladlaw and Reverend Blunt were in very great danger. However limited the flowers' protection against Dark Arts, it was a great deal better than having none at all.

Pattern felt the urgency of Reverend Blunt's situation. Her first objective must be to sink the row boat and thus postpone, if not prevent, the bird-watching expedition. But this would only delay his inevitable punishment. If she and Nate could discover the nature and source of Lady Hawk's power, then perhaps they could find some way of disabling it for good . . .

Pattern was anxious to hear Nate's ideas, particularly once he had learned of her encounter with Mr Grey and the book of ancient myths. Alas, it was not to be. Pattern had no sooner gone to collect Nate from below stairs than Mr Perks appeared.

'Ah, Penny, very good. Milady's pug has made a puddle in the drawing room, so I need you to fetch the

ammonia and lye. Quick as you can, now!'

Behind Mr Perks's back, Nate gave an apologetic grimace, but there was nothing he could do. Pattern Pendragon – dragon slayer, secret agent and aristocrat – must put her battle with supernatural villainy to one side, and go and mop up dog piddle.

CHAPTER FOURTEEN

∽∽ ∽∽

The unhappy object himself . . . is left to pine and sink in misery and contempt.

S. & S. Adams, *The Complete Servant*

∽∽ ∽∽

Clearing up after the pug cost Pattern precious time. She did not even have the chance to look for Nate again, for she heard Alfred calling out to William that he had been sent to find Reverend Blunt a sun hat. The clergyman must be preparing to leave for his excursion – Pattern could not delay her sabotage of the boat a moment longer.

The weather was turning hotter by the day, and as she made her way to the cove she saw how parched the landscape had become, showing none of the fresh greenness evident on their arrival. The fierce blue of the sky and the glare of the sun made her eyes ache. Yet the scene at the beach looked innocent enough. The row boat bobbed gently up and down at the end of the pier, the sand glittered silver-white, and the sea was calm. Although there was no mist this afternoon, there was no hint of the mainland to be seen either. Pattern had the unsettling notion that England itself had been spirited away, and that all on Cull were castaways, with nothing else in the world but boundless sea.

Pattern had intended to sink the boat with rocks, or else bash in its planks with a hammer she had taken from the stable yard. However, when she reached the vessel, she was dismayed to find that it was much larger and sturdier than she had remembered. What's more, she could already hear the Reverend Blunt's voice being carried towards her on the breeze. He and Mr Grey might arrive at any moment. And so Pattern was forced to make an impulsive, and possibly foolish, decision. Gritting her teeth, she clambered into the boat and made herself a hiding place under the fishing nets and canvas sacking.

Her refuge was smelly and stiflingly hot, but at least she did not have to wait long for Mr Grey and the Reverend, for they were only ten minutes behind her. Peeping out from the folds of canvas, she saw that Mr Grey was swathed in his customary black cloak, apparently immune to the heat. The Reverend, by contrast, was pink-faced and sweating copiously. He had left his coat behind, so even if Nate had managed to smuggle a snowdrop into its pockets, it would be of no use to him now. Pattern's own posy was of little comfort – it was highly unlikely the flowers would save her from drowning if she fell overboard.

It did not take the gentlemen long to settle into the boat and push off from the pier. The steward, despite his advanced age, pulled the oars with smoothness and strength. The boat headed a little way out to sea, then began to round the northern promontory of the cove,

heading to the neighbouring inlet.

Mr Blunt was peering through his binoculars at the seabirds. They seemed to be ordinary gulls to Pattern, but then she had no idea what the so-called Cull cormorant was supposed to look like.

From her hiding place under the canvas, Pattern managed to peep over the rim of the boat. The dark mass she had seen in the water previously was here again, about half a mile from the boat, though it was moving closer. A slight breeze had got up, carrying with it a faint but fishy smell. As she watched, the darkness began to froth up with dirty bubbles. Something was sticking out of the water – a branch of driftwood? Wreckage from a boat?

The branch was curved, and flexing like a muscle. It was oily green.

A shining grey-green coil.

A *tentacle*.

Pattern screwed up her eyes, feeling dizzy and sick. And when she looked again she felt that she was perhaps suffering from heatstroke, because there was

no tentacle,
but a woman's
head, breaking
the surface of
the waves.

It was the
head of a
very beautiful
woman.
Golden
haired, golden
skinned,
gleaming eyed.
It was not
Miss Hawk.

All the same, Pattern had a bad feeling about this. A very bad feeling indeed.

For the moment, the Reverend Blunt was oblivious. He was hunched over his seat, scribbling ornithological notes in his book. Mr Grey sat impassively, oars idle in his hands.

Meanwhile, the woman's head went under the water. When it re-emerged a second or two later, it was much closer to the boat. The breeze increased gustily, stirring the previously calm sea into choppy waves, and carrying with it the stench of seaweed and marshes. More bubbles frothed and foamed. Another three tentacles curled lazily upwards. The woman looked directly at Pattern and smiled. Her beautiful red lips opened to reveal two rows of greenish black-dripping fangs.

Pattern stifled a scream.

At the same moment, the Reverend Blunt looked out to sea – just as the woman closed her fanged mouth and the tentacles withdrew. All he saw was a golden head rising from the waves . . . Waves that were increasing in strength around the swimmer. She raised a hand and waved it in agitation.

'Good Lord! Look there – a young woman has got into difficulties in the water! Quick, man,' he told Mr Grey. 'We must row to the rescue. What an adventure, eh?' He rubbed his hands. 'Wait until Miss Hawk hears about *this*!'

It was clear he was already looking forward to regaling her with tales of his heroism. Pattern felt in the grip of a nightmare: a nightmare that had been lurking in the water this whole time. Something that had been circling the island ever since they'd got here. Something huge and dark, stinking of dead fish, with tentacles and fangs . . .

Mr Grey made a big display of attempting to row the boat closer to the woman, but his former ease with the oars seemed to have deserted him, and they were making little progress, to the Reverend Blunt's evident frustration. A cloud had come out of nowhere, covering the sun. With it, a chilly wind began to blow, and the waves became more vigorous.

Cursing the old man's incompetence, the Reverend Blunt began taking off his boots.

Pattern realized he was going to attempt to rescue the woman himself. At once, she threw off the nets and canvas and revealed herself.

'Please, sir,' she said to the astonished clergyman, 'you must stay out of the water at all costs. Please –'

she turned to Mr Grey – 'return us to the safety of the shore. I beg you, for pity's sake!'

'Idiot child,' the old man growled. 'Do you really think your meddling is going to be of any use?'

'So we have a stowaway!' exclaimed the Reverend, distracted. 'Really, the servants in this household are an utter disgrace. Insolence and insubordination at every turn!'

He prepared to lower himself into the water. Pattern attempted to drag him back, but he shook her off with disgust so that she sprawled backwards among the nets.

Both sea and sky were much darker now. Pattern could only watch helplessly from the bows as the clergyman began to swim towards the drowning damsel. Deaf to her pleas, Mr Grey was already rowing back to land.

The woman's head kept disappearing under the water and then bobbing up again in different places. Pattern was suddenly gripped by the idea that there were actually several different heads, attached to several different necks, belonging to whatever horror swam below. Like a thunderclap, an image came to her in black and red: the image of a monster she had once seen on a vase, back in the villa. *Six* heads, *twelve* tentacles! The waves were growing more tempestuous. The smell of fish slime and mud rot was even stronger . . .

Then suddenly, out of the broiling, swirling bubbles, Pattern cried out as a huge dark wave surged up as if from nowhere, and crashed over the clergyman's head.

A second wave roared towards their boat, sending it racing with unnatural speed towards the shore.

If Mr Grey had not seized her by the arm, Pattern would have fallen overboard as their vessel was tossed this way and that. Salt spray scoured her face; wind howled in her ears. It was several long moments before she was able to look back to see what had become of the unfortunate clergyman.

He was in the grip of three fleshy green tentacles. They were wrapped around his body, holding him aloft. His screams could barely be heard over the roar of the water, and the next instant he was plunged back down again into the sea's murky depths.

Meanwhile, the row boat had been spat on to the inlet's stony shore. Mr Grey nimbly disembarked and shook himself off. Pattern, her legs weak with terror, scrambled out after him. He helped her up on to the rocks, only letting go of her hand once they were some way up the cliff face.

'Do something!' Pattern implored him, as soon as she was able to speak. 'Stop this! He'll drown; he'll die; the monster—'

In answer, the old man merely shook his head and pointed to the water below.

The sea within the inlet had begun to froth and bubble and hiss. In a matter of moments, whirling and gurgling, the waves had churned themselves into a foamy circle, forming a whirlpool where none had been before.

A head suddenly appeared within it: not the woman's, but the Reverend's. He was spluttering and coughing, but very much alive. Rather than being sucked down into the centre to drown, he was carried around the edge of the whirlpool, as if on a watery treadmill. There was, however, no way of bringing him to shore. What made his plight all the more pitiful was the branch of scrub on an overhanging rock that was tantalizingly just out of reach. If he could only grab hold of it, he might have been able to haul himself out of the water. Yet it was an inch too far away. Round and round the water spun, and the Reverend spun with it.

It took all of Pattern's courage to look back out to sea. The water was growing calmer; the cloud was drifting away. The naked torso of a woman – three times as large as life, but as perfectly formed as one of the statues of goddesses back in the villa – rose from the waves. She had two graceful arms and wore a glittering ruby ring on her left hand. Six long necks sprouted from her shoulders; necks that were all muscle, sinuous as snakes, and crowned with six beautiful golden heads.

The six curved red lips opened in six hideous smiles, revealing twelve rows of rotting fangs.

Below her waist, where her legs should have been, the smooth pale flesh turned to green slime. She had the lower body of a giant octopus. Twelve tentacles

coiled upwards from the water, twisting and waving in what Pattern felt was a mocking salute. The creature raised the hand with the ring on it to her central head, and blew a kiss, before sinking back below the waves.

Of all the strange things she had ever witnessed, Pattern thought the sight of Mr Grey returning that blown kiss was perhaps the most shocking of all.

CHAPTER FIFTEEN

Think of what you have to do – of what must be done, and do it – even before it is wanted.

S. & S. Adams, *The Complete Servant*

'How could you?' Pattern demanded of Mr Grey. She was so angry she could scarcely get the words out. 'That poor man! Something must be done! He cannot be left there!'

But she got no answer. With a look of distaste, the old man removed a strand of seaweed from his shoulder. Then he turned on his heel and began to pick his way

along the path, back in the direction of the villa. Pattern hurried after him, still brimming over with protests.

Finally, at the edge of the wood overlooking the beach, he stopped and faced her. 'Why do you give a fig for Reverend Blunt? I am sure the priest would not lift a finger to save the likes of *you* – for you know his opinions on the lower classes.' He gave a snort. 'Yes, I may be old, but my eyes are sharp. I spied you peeping from the window while the gentry were at their luncheon.'

Anger made her reckless, but there was little point in keeping up the pretence that she was as noodle-brained as the rest of the party. 'The Reverend may be an unpleasant man, but nothing justifies such cruelty! I would say the same of Lady Hawk's other unfortunate gentlemen friends – Captain Vyne and Lord Charnly. So tell me: what was that . . . that creature?'

'*She* is Scylla. Show some respect!' He seemed genuinely offended.

That gave her pause. 'The same Scylla who appears in the book of Greek myths that Lady Hawk threw in the fire? The book with *your* name in it?'

He pursed his lips but did not answer.

Pattern brushed out her salt-stained, fish-stinking skirts, and tried to compose herself. She needed to keep her mind clear. 'It is curious: milady does not seem to like gentlemen very much. Yet she puts such trust in you.'

'That is because my lady knows I will never abandon her. She has made sure of that.' Mr Grey glanced out to sea where the dark shadow of Scylla was just discernible.

'Does Scylla attack whoever tries to leave the island?'

'Why would anyone want to leave? Isn't this place a paradise?' Mr Grey's tone had a bitter edge. 'Besides, Scylla would never hurt me. Even when she sleeps, in the hour before dawn, her dreams of me are kindly ones.'

Pattern did not understand it, yet, but intriguing associations were beginning to form in her mind. She, too, looked out from the cliffs. The abandoned row boat had somehow made its way from the inlet, borne

by the newly formed whirlpool, and was washed up on the beach below. Both its oars rested inside – Scylla clearly had tidy habits.

'I would never have thought something so monstrous could be so beautiful.'

He looked at her in surprise. 'You think her beautiful? Scylla?'

'I think,' Pattern said slowly, 'that she is like this island. Strange, corrupted and filled with loveliness as well as danger.'

'She was certainly lovely once.' Mr Grey cleared his throat. '*Cull* derives from a Cornish word. Do you know what it means?'

'The fishermen told me, yes: *loss*.'

'This island has been called many things, in many different languages, but the meaning is always the same. Because this isle is a place of lost things . . . and people.'

Pattern felt a chill breath at her neck. 'I do not want to be lost.'

'My lady's quarrel is not with you.'

'Because of my class? Or because of my sex?

'My lady only punishes those who deserve it.'

Pattern did not think this was said with much conviction. 'So our mistress is *not* like the old gods in the stories? She is never vindictive and vengeful, but always fair?'

The aged steward screwed up his eyes.

'She . . . she believes she acts for the best. And perhaps she does, some of the time. In truth, she is as likely to act out of boredom and mischief as from malice. I cannot help but think of the snowdrops. They have always flourished here, despite her efforts to uproot them. Perhaps it is a sign. Some things cannot be changed. Some things – some goodness – can never be entirely cut out.'

Then Lady Hawk might still have a capacity for mercy . . . Pattern hoped he was right.

'You have not told Lady Hawk of my meddling. You saved me from drowning, and dragged me back to the safety of the boat. Why is that?'

'Humph! I scarcely know myself. You are certainly a highly unsatisfactory housemaid: you are interfering

and insubordinate, and you shirk your work. However, I will allow these are not actual *crimes*.' He sighed. 'My loyalty must be to my lady. I will always protect her, and do her bidding. But this island already has its fill of prisoners. I do not wish to see an innocent soul among them.'

'Thank you,' Pattern said humbly. 'Does . . . does this mean the other servants are safe too? And the lady guests?'

He scowled. 'That depends. As long as they keep out of my lady's way – and mine.'

At least Pattern met with no reproach when she returned to the villa, for Mr Ladlaw's reading had been a lengthy one and was only just drawing to an end. This gave the ladies plenty of opportunity to ask questions and bestow compliments, while granting Pattern time for a much-needed wash and change of clothes. She had previously asked Mrs Robinson if she could miss the event, since she was making a study of *The Complete Servant* and would like to use the time to catch up on her own reading. Mrs Robinson, who privately feared *The Towers of Callabrio* was not entirely respectable, had been very happy to oblige.

'You're a sight for sore eyes!' Nate exclaimed as soon as Pattern rejoined her fellows in the servants' hall. Then, in lower tones: 'Whatever happened to our pact? Why did you leave a fellow high and dry, and half going out of his mind with worry?'

'There was hardly any time to think, let alone make plans,' she whispered back. 'The Reverend was about to put to sea, and—'

'Well, *you* missed a treat, make no mistake,' said Elsie, coming over to join them. 'Mr Ladlaw's story was ever so exciting, for there was a mad pirate ghost, and a wicked count, and a poor captive lady trying to make sense of it all. Mr Ladlaw has such a lovely speaking voice! He did all the accents and everything, and strode up and down waving his arms and such.'

'It must have been very entertaining,' Pattern said dutifully.

'We all thought it was as good as being at a play.

Except for Miss Smith, that is. She yawned throughout, and coughed and sneezed quite excessively, I thought – but then she does have a cold, poor thing, so perhaps that's why she did not pay the attention she should.'

'What did you think, Nate?'

'Oh, it was proper rip-roaring. But –' and here Nate gave Pattern a meaningful look – 'I warrant you could spin a yarn of your own, given half a chance.'

She looked at him confusedly.

'That story about the priest who went to sea?' he prompted.

'Oh, ah, yes – yes of course. It does not have a happy ending, I fear.'

Nate's face fell.

'In my, um, story, the priest tries to save a woman from drowning, but it is all a trick, because she is in truth a kind of monstrous octopus, who throws him into a magic whirlpool that traps him forever and ever. The – er – End.'

'Dear me, Penny, that wouldn't do at all,' said Elsie, shaking her head. 'Whoever would believe such absurdity? No, if you are going to write a tale of magic and adventure, then you had better read Mr Ladlaw's first, so you know how it is properly done.'

Nate looked ready to object to this, but Mrs Robinson had returned to the hall and was looking about her in a most suspicious manner. Perhaps she feared the corrupting influence of Mr Ladlaw's book had already begun to take hold.

'Seems to me, Mr Ladlaw's readers are going to be disappointed,' Nate said as soon as they had left the hall and could speak freely, 'and his tale of pirate ghosts and lady investigators will be his last.'

'I fear you're right.' Pattern rubbed her eyes. She was very dejected, and it took every ounce of her self-control not to let it show. 'We have to accept that we cannot protect Mr Ladlaw, or anyone else for that matter. Lady Hawk is too powerful, and her magic too unpredictable. The only course left to us is to persuade the gentleman to escape the island before she has time to strike.'

'He ain't going to listen to the likes of us. Not with Miss Hawk's smiles and her ma's music to befuddle his brain.'

'There are ways around that. Miss Hawk's mechanical charms are already failing, so next we must find a way for Mr Ladlaw to carry a snowdrop at tonight's concert. Once his mind is clear of magic, I believe we can convince him of the danger. The boat is waiting on the beach, and Mr Grey told me the sea monster sleeps in the hour before dawn. That is when we must make our escape. I do not like to leave the rest behind, but no one else on the island is in danger, if Mr Grey is to be believed.'

'You trust the old man?'

Pattern related her recent encounters with Mr Grey, and her suspicion that he served his mistress against his will. 'He said he would always protect his mistress. But I think if we were to attempt to flee he would not stand in our way. For why else would he have told me when Scylla sleeps? Why else has he not already told Lady Hawk that I am working against her? But I confess I do not know how to ensure Mr Ladlaw carries a snowdrop. If we hide a bloom in his clothes, he may change them or take them off – as happened with the Reverend.'

'Maybe us attempting to conceal the flowers ain't the answer, then. Maybe we should ask Mr Ladlaw to hide them himself.'

'How do you mean?'

'I mean, I'll play Cupid. I'll sidle up to the gent and whisper that Miss Hawk wants him to wear some of them snowdrops as a token of her affection, but to keep the flowers hidden, on account of her being so bashful and modest and the rest.'

'Yes, that could work. Perhaps tell him she wishes him to wear the flowers next to his heart? Or is that too much, do you think?'

'Not for a poet. It'll appeal to his romantic sensibilities, I reckon.' Nate rolled his eyes. 'You know what a sap these lovers can be – he'll moon over it in secret, like a girl with a wedding ring.'

Chapter Sixteen

Truth in speech must be accompanied by integrity and fidelity in all your dealings.

S. & S. Adams, *The Complete Servant*

What a curious gathering the house party had become: all ladies, save for one lone gentleman! As evening drew in, nobody enquired as to the whereabouts of the Reverend Blunt – not even his own sister, Honoria. As with the other male guests, it was as if he had never been. Pattern looked out over the darkening landscape and pictured the unfortunate clergyman spinning about in his whirlpool all through the night, and the endless days and nights to come.

Miss Hawk continued to twitch and creak and stutter, and both her speech and movements had noticeably slowed. Her mama let it be known that she had taken a medicine for her headache that did not agree with her, which aroused much insincere sympathy from the ladies, and very tender concern from Mr Ladlaw. By contrast, nobody enquired after Miss Smith's cold, despite her sneezing and sniffling. Poor lady! It was unlikely her rival's internal mechanisms could survive another day without winding. But another day was all Lady Hawk required, of course. She had despatched three suitors in as many days, no doubt the fourth was marked as Mr Ladlaw's last as a free man.

While Nate played Cupid with the snowdrops, Pattern turned to chemistry. The flowers might protect Mr Ladlaw from the mind-altering power of the music, but if he looked too restless and alert Lady Hawk would realize her enchantment had failed. Pattern needed to find something that would mimic the music's effect.

So she turned to her trusty sleeping draught, a home-brewed herbal concoction she had privately named Pendragon's Syrup of Somnolence.

She took the opportunity to slip into the dining room on the pretence of delivering a message to Mr Perks, and managed to put a couple of drops of the drug into Mr Ladlaw's wine glass without anyone noticing (such sleight of hand had been part of her training at the Silver Service, and she was glad of her hours of practice now). She hoped she had the dosage right: too much, and he would fall asleep; too little, and her efforts would be pointless. But although the gentleman yawned copiously throughout dessert, he did not start to snore in his seat, and by the conclusion of the evening concert he was as dozy-looking as the rest of the enchanted household.

The house was all abed by eleven, whereupon Pattern and Nate met in Lord Charnly's former bedchamber. Since the hour before sunrise when Scylla slept was their only opportunity to escape the island, they would have to be on the beach just before half past three. Furthermore, they needed to have enough time to persuade Mr Ladlaw of the danger and to allow for any unexpected interruption or delay. All in all, although they had planned to take the watch in shifts, and snatch a little sleep between times, both found they were far too on edge to rest.

'What'll you do once all this is over?' Nate asked.

Pattern felt a little uncomfortable. She could hardly tell Nate that she was actually the Countess of Annwn, and her home was an apartment in the royal castle of Elffinberg. She was still getting used to the idea herself.

'I will visit my good friend Eleri,' she said. 'And we will eat gingerbread until we feel sick, and stay up talking half the night.'

Oh, how she prayed this would happen!

'I like the sound of that. What about your parents, though?'

'They're dead.' Her mother and father had died in a shipwreck when fleeing Elffinberg in fear of the dragon But even if she could not mention the dragon, she felt she owed it to Nate to be as truthful as she could. So she explained that she believed her parents had been pastry-cooks, that they had drowned when she was a baby and that she had been raised in an orphanage before becoming a student at Mrs Minchin's Academy. Then she asked about Nate's own family.

'Well, my mother was a chambermaid, and she met my pa while in service. He were a footman to Lord Stannersly, who brought him over from his West Indies estate.'

Pattern might have guessed Nate's father had been born a slave, but she still found the idea very shocking, despite Nate's matter-of-fact tone. The two of them had already been through so much together that it was strange to realize they remained strangers in most regards. After all, there had been little time or opportunity to speak of anything that did not relate to Lady Hawk and her intrigues.

'But Pa died of a fever when I was little,' Nate continued, 'so Ma lives with her sister now. My aunt didn't want her to marry Pa, and made no bones about it. Caused quite a family rumpus! She don't like me so much either, to tell the truth. Being a betwixt-and-between . . . well, it can unsettle folk.'

'I think people need to be unsettled, sometimes,' said Pattern thoughtfully. 'And it may be that there are advantages to being neither one thing nor the other. You see the world from different angles.' She considered her experiences as both aristocrat and maidservant. 'It means you have to make your own path, and that can be rewarding, for all its difficulties.'

Nate smiled at her through the shadows. 'So what path are you on, Penny? I can guess it's full of secrets.'

'If we get out of here safely, I will tell you all about it.' Nate deserved the truth from her; of that she was now sure. 'No more mystery. That's a promise.'

*

It was still pitch black outside, but the time had come to begin their venture. Pattern splashed cold water over her tired face, still trying to think of the best way to break the bad news to Mr Ladlaw.

She trusted the snowdrop would restore some clarity to his thoughts, or at least weaken his resistance to the idea that he was in danger. Perhaps the fact that Mr Ladlaw had an author's colourful imagination would be in his favour. A man who could dream up tales of piratical ghosts might be more open than most to the idea that he was trapped on an enchanted island by a witch.

Since it was a warm night, Pattern found Mr Ladlaw sleeping outside the bedclothes. The open neck of his nightgown revealed that he had faithfully followed his beloved's instructions, as relayed to him by Nate: the snowdrops were bound by a ribbon to his chest. So far, so good. However, the lingering effects of her Syrup of Somnolence meant waking him was no easy task. In the end, she had to throw some water over his face too.

'Hell's teeth, girl! Have you lost your mind?' he

spluttered, eyes bleary with sleep, his dark tangle of hair sticking up in any number of directions. 'It's the middle of the night! What do you think you're doing?'

'Mr Ladlaw, sir, I am very sorry, but I need you to stay calm and believe me when I tell you that you are in very great danger and must leave this house and this island as soon as possible, in secret.'

'Good God! Is it a fire? Burglars? *Pirates?*'

'No, sir. It is altogether more complicated. I will try to explain, but first I must ask: what do you remember of your last few days on the island, sir?'

Groggily, he ran his hands through his hair. 'Well, Miss Hawk has been as charming as always. She has borne the other gentlemen's unwelcome attentions with admirable patience and restraint.'

'You remember the other gentlemen then, sir?'

'Of course. There was . . . hmm . . . a soldier who fancied himself a ladies' man, and a clergyman with absolutely no literary taste whatsoever. And some fellow with a scowl, who kept blathering on about pheasants . . . How odd – I feel I know their names perfectly well, yet

they have become fearfully muddled.' As he rubbed his eyes, some of his bewilderment cleared, and he began to be more aware of the impropriety of their situation. 'What are you, anyway – a scullery maid? Who are *you* to discuss Miss Hawk and her suitors?'

Despite herself, Pattern felt a little aggrieved at being mistaken for such an inferior servant. 'I am a third housemaid, sir, but I also wish to be your friend, since I fear you have made a powerful enemy.'

'Pooh! What enemies could a poet possibly have? Our words are balm to the troubled soul, not incitement to violence! In any case, I am not accustomed to making friends with servants, least of all those who ambush me in the middle of the night with mad warnings and impertinent questions.' He reached for his dressing gown. 'Enough of this nonsense. I really must insist you leave.'

'Please wait, sir. Wait and think a moment. Miss Hawk had four suitors, of which you are one. Yet you are the only gentleman left in this house. So where are those other gentlemen now? When did you last encounter them?'

This gave him pause. 'I – well, let's see. We were having a picnic and then . . . I think there was a walk . . . the scenery was supposed to be most inspiring . . . if only I could have kept myself from getting lost! Or was it Miss Hawk who was lost? I cannot tell. It was all very confusing. But then . . . then . . .' His face changed. 'My God – I remember it now – I was fighting a duel. A *duel*! Or did I dream this? It must have been a nightmare, I'm sure of it.'

'No dream, sir. You fought a duel with the Reverend Blunt.'

'That pompous windbag? I refuse to believe it.'

'Look at your arms; they bear the marks of your battle.'

Mr Ladlaw rolled up the sleeve of his nightgown and beheld the scratches and scrapes and specks of dried blood that covered his skin, first in astonishment, then horror.

'Sweet heavens. I didn't *kill* the man, did I?'

'No, sir. He suffered a different fate.'

'I don't understand.' Mr Ladlaw put his head in his hands. 'I am a lover, not a fighter. I have not fenced since my school days! My poor head . . . it is such a jumble of impossible things. Perhaps it is the heat. Yes, that must be it. I am not accustomed to the climate, and it is making me ill.'

'Indeed, sir, the climate here is very unusual. Were you not surprised to find olive groves and lemon trees so close to the Cornish coast?'

'I am no more a gardener than I am a duellist, but I suppose you do have a point. Oh dear,' he said weakly, 'I do not feel at all well. Is that what happened to the other gentlemen? Perhaps they were taken ill and have gone away for medical attention. It seems to me we must all be suffering from a fever of the brain.'

'That is not a bad way of describing it, sir. But tonight you are in your right mind, I assure you. To this end, I am going to show you what befell poor Captain Vyne. So I must ask you to please look into the mirror by the fireplace, and endeavour to stay calm, however shocking the image you see there.'

Mr Ladlaw pressed his hands to his face anxiously. 'Why? What's happened to me? Was I badly scarred in the duel?'

'No, sir. Thus far, you are unharmed.'

He had already got up and hastened to the mirror. 'Then what –'

He started back with a gasp of horror. There was the anguished face of Captain Vyne, holding out his hands in desperate appeal on the other side of the glass. Until now, it was only Pattern and Nate who had seen him.

'What madness is this?'

'Not madness, sir. Magic. It is the magic of Lady Hawk.'

He stared at her, mouth agape. 'M-magic?'

'Lord Charnly and Reverend Blunt are also trapped, though in different prisons. You will be next, unless you trust me to help you escape.'

'B-b-but –'

'Please, sir, we are already running out of time. I will wait outside the door while you get dressed – quickly

now! – and I will endeavour to explain as we make our way out of here.'

Pattern was rigid with impatience by the time the gentleman emerged, fully dressed, but as dishevelled as he was agitated. Nate met them in the corridor. While Pattern had been persuading Mr Ladlaw of the gravity of his situation, Nate had been collecting some essentials to add to Pattern's bag: a posy of snowdrops, flasks of water, food, weatherproof clothing . . . and a pistol from the gun room.

Mr Ladlaw goggled at him. 'Is that the *hall boy*? This night gets stranger by the minute. I am to be saved from my magical doom by a confederacy of urchins!'

'We have not saved you yet, sir,' said Pattern grimly, and took the liberty of taking him by the arm to hustle him along more quickly. They would leave through the back stairs and the servants' entrance.

And she was right to be worried, for at the end of the corridor, window-lit by moonshine, the figure of Miss Hawk had appeared.

CHAPTER SEVENTEEN

Delays are dangerous.

S. & S. Adams, *The Complete Servant*

Miss Hawk was blocking their way to the stairs. Although her dress and features were as sweetly pretty as ever, she could no longer have passed as an ordinary young woman. The light in her eyes burned with inhuman brightness. Her body was rigid, moving only in jerks. Stiffly, she pointed a finger at the three of them in accusation.

'You,' she said, in a voice that sounded like the

grinding of metal gears. 'You. Have. Unmade. Me.'

'Heaven preserve us!' Mr Ladlaw quavered. 'She . . . It . . . This cannot be . . .'

The doll moved forward in fits and starts. Its plight was not just that of an instrument that was winding down. When Pattern had jammed the brass key from the clock into the doll's back, she must have inflicted lasting damage. The rusty creaks and clanking from within spoke of some terrible internal collapse.

'You,' she said again. 'You. Have. Unmade. Me. You – un – made – me. Me – un – made – I. Unmake. You. Unmake you – un – make –'

Mr Ladlaw began to gasp and quake. Pattern tried to be sympathetic: he had received a great many shocks in a very short space of time. He was now faced with his former Heart's Delight, his Dearest Beloved, in the midst of a mechanical breakdown. Still, Pattern found herself wishing he would be just a *little* less feeble. Poets were all well and good, but, given the circumstances, a man of action might be more useful.

Miss Hawk's hands were outstretched, and from

under their pearly nails, metal
prongs suddenly
sprung. Curls of
acrid-smelling smoke
rose from her nostrils
and her ears. Her teeth
clashed. Her eyes spat cold blue
sparks. Every joint moved stiffly
and slowly, but with horrible
purpose.

The three of them
backed away.

'I – un – make – you!'

They had reached the wall; there was nowhere else
to go. Miss Hawk's pronged nails stretched out towards
them. She was only six feet away now. A blue flame
crackled in her eyes; she ground her teeth and sparks
flew.

Pattern plunged her hands into the bag of supplies,
but Nate got there first. With shaking hands, he drew
out the pistol, aimed and fired. Bullets ripped into Miss

Hawk's bodice, and she let out a rusty shriek. More smoke plumed from her body, wire coils and sparking cogs sprang out of her chest, but although she was slowed she did not stop.

'U-u-u-u! N-n-n-n! M-m-m! A-a-a-a!'

Nate crossed himself. Mr Ladlaw quivered and moaned. Pattern grasped her knitting needles, ready to thrust them into the doll's mechanics in a last-ditch attempt to jam her workings once and for all.

'Aiiiiiiiiiiieeeeeeeeeee!'

Something crashed into the back of Miss Hawk's head with a thunderous clang. Again and again and again. Blue sparks fizzed and flashed. Smoke billowed. Joints shrieked. Finally, the metal woman crumpled to the ground, where she lay twitching and blinking, but otherwise motionless.

Standing over her prostrate body was Miss Smith, a poker in her hands.

'I've been wanting to do that for some time,' she said, only a little breathlessly.

*

Miss Smith followed her heroics by blowing her nose, noisily, on the hem of Miss Hawk's gown. It transpired that her head cold had performed the same function as Mr Ladlaw's snowdrops and Nate and Pattern's wax plugs. Since Miss Smith's ears had been blocked along with her nose, that evening, for the first time since coming to the island, Lady Hawk's enchanted music had not been able to fog her brain.

'Tonight I felt so much clearer in my mind. Yet at the same time I began to suffer a mounting sense of dread. Lying in bed, I became convinced that something was terribly wrong with all of us here. Unable to sleep, my head full of strange fancies, I resolved to go outside to take the air. It was on my way downstairs that I found you and that – that – *thing*. How did you come to be attacked by it? What do you know about this place? Are any of you able to account for these happenings?'

'I will do my best, miss, but first I must ask you to come with us, as quick as you can, to a place of greater safety.' In truth, Pattern was surprised the sound of gunshots had not roused the house, or brought Lady

Hawk storming through the corridors. The night sky was already beginning to lose its inkiness; they were close to running out of time.

As the four of them hurried down the back stairs and out through the garden, Pattern gave a brief explanation of the Dark Magic of Lady Hawk. 'I do not know exactly who or what she is,' Pattern said, 'but I suspect she came into her powers in the distant past – like the pagan gods and monsters depicted in the art of her house, and the book of myths she took from you.'

'My *Tales from Ovid*?' Miss Smith looked a little faint. 'Then we are in a deal of trouble. None of those stories end well, you know.'

'Have you read them all?' Pattern was very anxious to learn the history of Glaucus and Scylla.

'No,' Miss Smith said regretfully. 'I am familiar with the more famous ones – such as Orpheus and Eurydice, for example – but I had barely started on the volume when Lady Hawk took it from me. I can tell you that they are all tales of betrayed love and transformation.'

'Transformation?' Pattern echoed.

'Yes, of men and women turned into beasts or plants or monsters for crimes against the gods. Now, of course, I understand why this might appeal to our host.' She bit her lip. 'You know, I remember seeing the statue of Lord Charnly in the garden, and thinking there was something uniquely horrid about it. But I could not work out why. Similarly, I have met stupid girls, and sly girls, but none as empty-headed as Miss Hawk. How she irked me! She was like those ninnies in popular romances, existing only as decoration, with no original thought at all and no natural ability except that of pleasing men. So perhaps it is not surprising she is revealed to be an entirely artificial construct.'

'Thankfully, not *all* gentlemen wish ladies to be merely decorative,' said Pattern, with a significant glance at Mr Ladlaw, who was stumbling along, pasty-faced and glass-eyed. 'The heroine of *his* novel is every bit as commanding and resourceful as a sensible reader could wish.'

'One can only hope,' said Miss Smith, somewhat tartly, 'Mr Ladlaw receives the acclaim he deserves.'

'We have to save him from the dangers of this island and its mistress first. She is intent on his destruction.'

'Yes, and what a tragic loss for Literature that would be!'

Pattern was a little surprised. She detected something sarcastic in Miss Smith's tone. But it was only natural that Miss Smith was feeling bruised by events. She would soon come to realize that Mr Ladlaw's infatuation with Miss Hawk was through no fault of his own. No doubt time would heal the lovers' rift.

And, though it would help if Mr Ladlaw had made some romantic gesture or apology, Pattern supposed it was not possible in his current condition. Nate had to keep prodding him in the back to ensure he kept the pace.

'Get a move on,' Nate said, exasperated. 'You're the poor sap Lady Hawk wants to make into mincemeat, but we'll suffer as well if she catches us helping you. I reckon we've got ten minutes left to pile into that boat, or else it will be too late to push off, and then the octopus lady will be eating all of us for breakfast.'

This speech did not have the stimulating effect he wished, for Mr Ladlaw gave a moan of terror and came to a complete stop. Pattern seized his arm, in an attempt to drag him onwards.

'Sir! You really *must* get a hold of yourself. Now we have reached the wood, we are really very close. For the beach is just below – look.'

'N-n-not there . . . There.' With a shaking hand, he pointed to the trees.

A tiger had slunk out of the wood. It was snarling, teeth bared.

They moved together instinctively. The tiger, hackles raised, padded closer. It was very different to the poor mangy creature Pattern had seen at the zoological gardens. It was glossy and muscled, rippling with savage beauty and strength.

Nate took out his posy of snowdrops and brandished them at the beast. It immediately lowered its head and purred as sweetly as a tabby cat, but did not move its position. Next it was joined by a lynx and a wolf. The

sound of hooves made the three swing round, only to see their path back to the villa was blocked by an enormous shire horse and a shining black panther.

'Shoot them!' said Mr Ladlaw. 'You have a weapon, don't you? Shoot a way through!' He dived for the bag.

Nate snatched it away. 'Did you never notice how all the animals around this place are male?'

'What's that got to do with anything?' snapped Mr Ladlaw.

'Think about it. What with all the jiggery-pokery going on, I wouldn't be too surprised if them beasts were once like you or me.'

'Pshaw,' said Mr Ladlaw.

At the horizon, the sky was beginning to turn grey.

'Not a chance worth taking, sir,' said Pattern. She was sure Nate was right.

'No indeed,' murmured Miss Smith, staring into the impassive yellow eyes of the panther. 'How could we live with ourselves?'

In any case, there were now far more animals than bullets. It was the same mix of domestic and wild creatures as the pack that had hunted Lord Charnly to his doom. Above them, a motley flock of birds – parrots and songbirds, as well as birds of prey – swooped and dived. The birds flew so close that beaks snapped in their ears, and talons raked their hair. If any beast got dangerously aggressive, thrusting the snowdrops at the animal turned it docile in an instant. But they did not move out of their way. A milky light had begun to suffuse the sky; dawn was fast approaching, and Scylla would be waking from her rest.

They were not being harmed, but they *were* being herded.

Herded through the olive groves, past the plantations of orange and lemon trees and stands of cypresses . . . Herded over the hills and towards the summer house . . .

Miss Smith found the walk particularly hard going, since she was in her shabby nightclothes, with only worn-down slippers to protect her feet. Still, she was in better spirits than Mr Ladlaw, who continued to wring his hands and bewail the misery of his lot. 'If I

am to face my doom, then at least I will face it with a sound mind,' she said. 'I have had quite enough of thinking in a fog. Moreover, my cold is much better. I am very glad not to have to battle an immortal enchantress whilst my nose is dripping. It puts one at such a disadvantage.'

Pattern could think of no advantages to their situation whatsoever.

Nate glanced at her doleful face, and nudged her in the ribs. 'They say that if tin-mining was to fail, Cornwall could reinvent itself as a place for rich folks to go on their holidays. I can't see it happening, meself.'

She did not laugh, but she *did* feel glad that he was with her.

As dawn broke, they reached the hill with the summer house overlooking the sea.

Gilded by the morning light, the building appeared more like a temple than ever. The white marble columns and high domed roof were flushed with the rosy hue of dawn. The sun's rays flashed from the statue of a nymph on her pedestal and on the golden crown of

Lady Hawk, who stood at the foot of the steps with bare arms, flowing white robes and unbound hair.

'What have you done with my darling daughter?' she asked.

CHAPTER EIGHTEEN

❧ ❧

How preposterous it is to hear a woman say, 'It shall be done' – 'I will have it so!'

Mrs Taylor, *Practical Hints to Young Females*

❧ ❧

Under the dome were the ladies from the house party – Honoria Blunt, Alicia and Adele Lane, and the Dowager. Ranged behind them were the female servants of the household.

All were in their nightclothes. All wore strange smiles on their faces. All were unnaturally still and calm.

Glaucus Grey, grim-faced as ever and wrapped in his black cloak, stood immediately behind his mistress.

Far out to sea, Pattern glimpsed six golden heads watching from the waves.

The throng of animals settled themselves on the grassy slopes around the hill. They did not scratch or sniff or roll about or do any of the things ordinary animals might do. They were as still and silent as the assembled humans.

'Well?' Lady Hawk demanded in theatrical tones. 'Where is my sweet Cassandra?'

There was an uncomfortable pause.

'She – she wasn't your daughter, milady,' Pattern said bravely, since nobody else seemed inclined to speak. 'Not unless you're made of cogs and wires too.'

Lady Hawk descended the steps.

'Poor Cassandra is one of a kind: the last, and greatest, work of that master craftsman Pygmalion. It will take a great deal of time and trouble to put her back to rights.'

'If you do, then you should find better use for such a

miracle of science than luring gentlemen to their doom.'

Lady Hawk pursed her lips. 'What a bother you've caused me, little Penelope! Glaucus tells me someone has been digging up my moly flowers. I suppose that must be you and your friend too. How did you get around Alasdair, I wonder?'

'Alasdair?'

'A one-time Scottish laird, and a most slippery character.'

Nate and Pattern exchanged looks. Alasdair had to be the snake that guarded the snowdrops. No wonder it had tartan scales and a taste for Scottish folk tunes! Here was further proof, if proof were needed, that the island animals had been human once.

The sorceress clicked her fingers and the snowdrops they were carrying flew through the air and into her hands. She wound the flowers into her hair with a complacent smile.

'The original Penelope, you know, also appeared very quiet and dutiful, and useful around the house. Her weaving was remarkable. But then all the while she was picking and pulling at the thread, undoing everything as she went along . . .' Lady Hawk shook her head regretfully. 'The difference is, of course, that the first Penelope was spoiling her *own* work. You, on the other hand, have attempted to unravel mine.'

Pattern swallowed. 'I do not much care for your work, milady.'

'Me neither,' Nate piped up. 'It ain't respectable, turning people's heads to porridge, jinxing gentlemen right and left.'

'Not *all* gentlemen,' said Lady Hawk, fixing her gleaming dark eyes on Mr Ladlaw. 'Not yet.'

Mr Ladlaw sank to his knees. 'P-please, I b-beg you – Honourable Madam! Gracious Lady! If I have unwittingly caused offence, or neglect of some kind, then I will do everything, *everything*, in my power to make it up to you. I swear. I swear!'

Pattern looked at Miss Smith, expecting her to plead for mercy on her lover's behalf. But Miss Smith was watching quite coolly, her arms folded across her chest.

'Do you know why your fellow suitors have been

punished?' Lady Hawk enquired.

Mr Ladlaw tearfully shook his head.

'Then I think it is time to enlighten you.'

Mr Grey brought out a high-backed golden chair and set it at the foot of the steps. He followed this with a glass of champagne on a silver platter. Lady Hawk settled into the seat with a sigh of satisfaction, and took a sip from the glass. The blank-eyed women behind her, and the animals spread out before her, continued to look on with rapt attention.

'Lord Charnly wished to knock down an old woman's cottage so he could build a hunting lodge. He had his henchmen drag the poor lady out from her bed in the dead of night – one of those brutes was his valet Stokes, by the way. Abandoned in the cold, the woman died soon after. No doubt Lord Charnly feels excessively chilly and stiff inside his marble cladding . . . but it is more comfortable than the morgue, wouldn't you say?

'Captain Vyne broke hearts, destroyed reputations and ruined lives, all because he could not resist the dazzle of his own charm. Now he is a prisoner of his reflected beauty. I suspect he is considerably less proud of it now.

'The Reverend Blunt stole from widows and orphans, under the guise of offering them a helping hand. How fitting, then, that he should whirl round and round, helplessly, with the chance of salvation always just outside his reach . . .

'So there you have it. There are many scoundrels I might have chosen to torment, but I consider those who dishonour women to be the blackest villains of all.' Here her expression turned dark. 'Moreover, these gentlemen were particularly suited to my games – for have I not made the punishments fit their crimes in a splendidly neat fashion?'

At once, the women assembled behind her, servants and ladies alike, broke into polite applause.

'Will the gents be fixed like that forever?' Nate asked. He looked a little queasy.

'Oh no,' came the reply. 'Only for as long as it amuses me. Then I shall set them free – save for one, who I will keep for my collection of pets. I have not yet decided

who it shall be. Lord Charnly would make a splendid bull, with that lowered black brow of his. But then I am also tempted by the idea of doleful Mr Ladlaw as a raven. I'm sure his cawing would be highly poetical.'

'But – but what crime has Mr Ladlaw committed?' Pattern asked.

'Like the others, a crime against womankind. Perhaps Miss Smith would care to enlighten you.'

'Miss Smith? But she is in love with him!'

Miss Smith snorted. 'Not in a hundred years. Not in a hundred *thousand*.'

Pattern felt quite confounded. Foolish too. How could she have got this so wrong?

'We *were* friends,' Miss Smith conceded. 'I was a governess for his younger brothers and sisters, you see. I wanted to write, to make an independent life for myself, and he encouraged me. Such wonderful letters he sent me, full of praise and promises! He told me I would have a far better chance of publication if he took my writing to his editor friends and presented it as being the work of a gentleman. I believed him. I trusted him. First with the poetry, but then with my novel – even though I particularly wanted it to be published under my own name.'

'*You* wrote the Towers of Whatsit?' Nate was saucer-eyed. 'I'd never have guessed it was by a lady, it were that good.'

'And there we have it,' said Miss Smith sharply. 'The ignorant prejudice of men laid bare.' She sighed. 'Anyhow, Mr Ladlaw said the publisher told him my book would do much less well if people believed it to be by a lady novelist. We should wait, and only reveal its true author once it was a success. So I waited, and I waited, and watched as my book became a minor sensation. Yet my authorship was never revealed. Instead, Mr Ladlaw took all the money, and all the acclaim, and told anyone who heard my claims that I was soft in the head, and madly in love with him to boot. I lost my position as a governess, and was thrown on the charity of my cousins Frederick and Honoria Blunt. They do not like me, and treat me like a servant – but it is them or the workhouse, so what else can I do?'

'Precisely!' said Lady Hawk. 'Such gross injustice must not be allowed to stand.'

'That may be so,' said Miss Smith with spirit, 'but I do not see why it should be up to you to correct it. *I* am the injured party after all.'

'Yes, and you are poor and powerless. I am not. I have lived for a great many years, and over time all sorts of men have washed up on this island, making great claims and promises, all of which have proved false. What a tedious mess men have made of running the world! Why should I not amuse myself by redressing the balance, just a little? Wouldn't you agree, ladies?'

The assembled women clapped their hands with vigorous enthusiasm.

'Quite right,' murmured Miss Lane.

'So true,' said the Dowager Duchess.

'Very instructive,' said Mrs Robinson.

'Hear, hear,' said Jane.

Pattern frowned. It seemed to her that Lady Hawk's claims to advance the female cause were somewhat undermined by magicking a group of women into agreeing with her every word.

Judging by Miss Smith's expression, she thought the same. 'When all's said and done,' the novelist said, 'I am inclined to think that Mr Ladlaw has suffered enough.'

'How do we know *any* of them have?' Lady Hawk indicated the menagerie before her. 'Dumb animals can hardly tell us how their morals and manners have improved.'

'Then turn one of them back so he can speak for himself,' said Pattern, with new boldness. 'Let us hear from one of your former victims. Let us hear from Mr Henry Whitby.'

'Who?' asked Lady Hawk, wrinkling her brow. Nate and Miss Smith also looked at Pattern in confusion. (Mr Ladlaw was far too busy wringing his hands to do anything much.)

'Henry Whitby. He was at your island party in Italy, but never came home. He is the reason I joined your household. I am looking for him on behalf of his guardian, who is exceedingly upset at his loss.' Pattern hardly knew where the authority in her voice came

from. She was feeling very small and shaky inside. 'A rather plump young gentleman . . . with a habit of losing at cards?'

'Ah yes, I remember now. I believe he defrauded an elderly spinster out of her life savings, all so he could pay a gambling debt. He was in every way lazy, greedy and deceitful.'

'But capable of change, I am sure. Won't you please restore him to his human form so he can plead his case and prove how well he has learned his lesson?'

'Hmm. After a certain amount of time spent living as animals, I am afraid my guests are apt to forget their human selves. As such, there is no way of turning them back. But I suppose Mr Whitby was my most recent acquisition, so it *may* not be too late . . . I tell you what, little Penelope – if you can find Mr Whitby, you can have him. But you will have only one chance to choose. If you get it wrong, then Mr Whitby must stay as he is.'

'Thank you, milady.'

Pattern smoothed down her skirts and surveyed the assembled birds and beasts, thoughts racing. She

concentrated on keeping her breathing slow and steady,
so to concentrate better. She had everything to play for
and much to prove.

Lazy . . . greedy . . . deceitful.

Lady Hawk assigned animal identities according
to both character and looks, if her musings on Lord

Charnly as a bull and Mr Ladlaw as a raven were a guide.

Pattern walked among the animals. Such an abundance of furs and scales and feathers! She had toured London's zoological gardens not long before joining Lady Hawk's household, but this was an entirely different experience, for the creatures were so silent and still that they might as well have been stuffed and sitting in glass cases in a museum.

'Please, might I have a closer look at the sloth?'

Lady Hawk clicked her fingers, and the sloth ambled forward. It was shaggy and grey with squinty black eyes.

'Now the pig with the spots.'

Another click of the fingers and the black-and-white-patched pig trotted to join the sloth. Pattern remembered batting away its snout in the dining room.

'Finally, the snake – not the one who lives by the snowdrops, but that one there. The green one, please.'

She surveyed her three candidates: lazy sloth, greedy pig, deceitful snake.

What did she know about Henry Whitby? That he

was small and stout, with bulging eyes. That he lost money on gambling, and lied about it. That he drank too much. That his favourite food was oysters . . .

'I don't suppose it would be possible,' she asked, 'to procure some oysters?'

It was. A wave of Lady Hawk's hand, and Mr Grey produced another silver platter, this time with a dish of oysters on it. Pattern put the oysters down on the grass. The sloth and the snake regarded them blankly. But the pig eagerly trotted forward and began slurping them up from their shells.

'That one,' Pattern said, and she could not quite keep the tremble from her voice. 'That is Henry Whitby.'

CHAPTER NINETEEN

Consider your business as a pleasurable amusement and you will make it so.

S. & S. Adams, *The Complete Servant*

There was a long and anxious wait. Then Lady Hawk began to applaud. So did the spellbound ladies. Nate and Miss Smith whooped. Even Mr Ladlaw managed a sickly smile.

'Very good, little Penelope. Very good! You have caused me a deal of trouble, yet I cannot help but be amused by you. It has been many years – centuries –

since anyone has been so wise to my tricks.'

'Thank you, milady.'

'Oh, call me Circe, do. We need not stand on ceremony any longer. You know, I am half tempted to keep you on this island. I think I should quite enjoy having a maid as quick-witted as you.'

'Thank you, Mrs Circe, ma'am – but I am not in need of employment.' Pattern licked her dry lips. 'I only need to return Mr Whitby to his relations.'

'How tiresome of you. Very well – let us see what the young man has to say for himself.'

The woman who had been Lady Cecily Hawk and the Contessa Cecilia di Falco, and was now simply Circe, rose from her chair and came to where the pig was still gobbling its treats. She rapped it three times on its bristly snout.

A plump and anxious-looking young man, in muddy clothes that had once been exceedingly fine, was suddenly crouched, snuffling, on the grass.

'Oink!' he squealed. 'Grumph!' he grunted.

He rubbed his snub nose and snuffled some more.

His eyes darted about as he rose unsteadily to his feet. 'Gr – umph – oink – where is she? Where is my love? My – umph – darling Cassiphone?'

'She goes by the name of Cassandra these days,' said Circe. 'And I'm afraid she's indisposed.'

His eyes filled with tears. 'Alas! All my suffering would be worth it, if I could only win a smile from her lips!'

'What makes you think you are worthy of her? You cheated a poor spinster to pay a gambling debt. You have frittered away your fortune, wasted your education, disappointed your relatives and betrayed your friends.'

Henry Whitby hung his head. 'I know. All this is true. I can only say that I was determined to be a better man for your daughter's sake. Her goodness made me ashamed of myself. Her sweetness inspired me to better things.'

'And what if I were to say that all this goodness and sweetness and the rest was merely a masquerade? Your love for Cassandra is not real, because Cassandra is not real. She is little more than a moving, talking statue. The feelings she arouses in you are as much of an enchantment as that piggy skin you have been wearing this past year. If you were to leave my island, you would forget her charms in an instant.'

'Then – then I will search and search until I find someone who *is* real, and worthy of my love. Someone to inspire truly noble thoughts and feelings. Someone to help transform me into my best self. I shall not rest until I become worthy of such a woman.'

'Hmm,' said Circe, settling back down on her golden chair. 'I am not convinced. Beauty withers; charm dwindles; love fades. I think you would soon go back to your old ways without the fear of magical punishment, or hope of magical love.'

'Real love is not magical,' said Pattern, 'but it is powerful nonetheless.'

'Ah! So you are a romantic, then, little Penelope!'

No, thought Pattern, I am not romantic. I am practical. But love and romance are not the same thing. Love had made her parents give up everything they had to embark on a dangerous sea voyage in order to

give their daughter the chance of a better life. Love had compelled Pattern to rush up a mountain and fight a dragon to save her dearest friend. Love had brought Nate's parents together, in spite of the 'rumpus' it caused.

Circe shook her head, smiling. 'I should warn you that true love is even more dangerous than the magical kind. It is as likely to turn people into monsters as angels, I fear. It certainly never did me any good.' And here, Pattern was interested to see, she looked sidelong at Glaucus Grey.

'Mostly, however, it just makes people dull. There was a man from my past, a travelling man; Odysseus was his name. He was the first but not the last to abandon me. You can read all about it in Homer, if you are so minded, though bear in mind that Homer was a man, so his account of the affair is very partial, and not entirely to be trusted. Anyhow, Odysseus was exceedingly clever (if not as clever as me) and a great storyteller. So entertaining! Alas, rather than choose to spend a merry immortality with me, he went back to his wife – the dreary and dutiful Penelope – and thus ended his adventures. She was his true love, apparently. I still find it surprising.'

Pattern was shocked into silence. Although she had guessed Circe was much older than she appeared, it was still quite a thing to hear she was *immortal*. It was clear she had been exacting vengeance on men for centuries. And what was this vengeance for – the betrayal of abandonment? Odysseus, she said, was the first. But were there others? And what had become of them? She looked between Mr Grey, who stood there with his head hung low, and Circe, brooding on her throne.

Finally, the enchantress stretched and sighed. 'Dear me – time does drag when you have limitless supplies of it! Perhaps we would all benefit from a new form of entertainment. A wager to keep us on our toes.

'Somewhere on my island, little Penelope, there is a token of true love that once belonged to me. If you can find it, then I will release Mr Whitby along with the other gentlemen and everyone else on this island. If not, then Mr Whitby will return to his porcine form,

Mr Ladlaw will receive the punishment I planned for him and everyone else will be compelled to spend the next few decades or so on Cull, providing me with all the amusement and distraction I could wish for.

'Do you accept the challenge?'

Of course Pattern accepted the challenge. There was no other choice.

The idea of spending the next few decades a prisoner on Cull struck fear into her bones. Thus far, Circe had been a liberal mistress to her servants, but it was easy to see that once boredom and irritation set in she would resort to all sorts of unpleasant tricks. Who knows what fresh humiliations and entrapments were in store? They might spend whole weeks fighting pointless duels, entire months chasing phantoms through the mist . . .

In the meantime, Circe seemed much invigorated by her latest scheme. She clapped her hands and remarked, repeatedly, how much fun they would all have.

'I'm helping Pattern,' Nate announced.

'Are you indeed? So chivalry is not yet dead. Well, I suppose I'll allow it. The more the merrier, after all! What about you, Mr Ladlaw? Would you like to stay here and keep me company, or gad about with these urchins?'

Mr Ladlaw blinked. Neither prospect was an enticing one. 'I, um, would like to assist with the, er, quest, my lady. To be, um, useful. And helpful. And make amends.' He attempted an ingratiating smile.

'Well, mind that you *are* helpful – if you are not, there will be consequences. Mr Grey will be there to keep an eye on you all, and provide any little thing you might need. You see how reasonable I am: I wish the wager to be a fair one.'

Mr Grey did not look at all happy about this, and even opened his mouth as if to object, but after a look from Circe he lapsed into silence. Pattern had hoped that he might intervene at some point, or give some sign that he was ready to oppose his mistress, but it seemed he'd spoken the truth when he'd said that he would never actively defy her. She wondered again why

he might have been doomed to serve the enchantress for all eternity.

'What about me?' Miss Smith asked.

'You, my dear, can entertain us by reading from your novel while we wait. Mr Whitby can read out the gentlemen's parts, and it will all be highly diverting. A literary salon! I have, after all, known a deal of poets and writers over the course of my life. My critical opinion will be invaluable.'

Circe gave them until noon to complete the challenge.

Pattern hoped this was a good sign. The enchantress was not, after all, entirely unreasonable. She clung to Mr Grey's words. *I cannot help but think of the snowdrops. They have always flourished here, despite her efforts to uproot them. Perhaps it is a sign. Some things cannot be changed. Some things – some goodness – can never be entirely cut out.*

Could it be true? Her games with the gentlemen were surely every bit as despicable as her victims' crimes. But if Pattern entertained Circe sufficiently, would she pardon them?

Pattern began proceedings by drawing Nate away for a private conference.

'You know what Circe's token of love is, don't you?' Nate said. 'I can tell by the glint in your eye.'

'Identifying it is one thing; getting it is quite another. But, yes, I think I do. I am fairly certain it is a ring.'

'Like a wedding band? Lord. Who'd ever be daft enough to marry a witch? One cross word over breakfast and she'd turn you into a toast rack! But something that small could be *anywhere*. Why, we could search all year and hardly cover half the nooks and crannies on this island.'

'It is not on the island proper, though. It is in its waters.' Pattern described her encounter with Scylla more fully. 'I am sure it is Scylla's ring.'

'But Circe said the love-token belonged to her. Did Scylla steal it, then – reach out of the water and grab it off her with one of them tentacles?'

'Either way, Circe is testing us.'

'Ho, you don't say! Fighting a monster-octopus-lady ain't no joke.'

Pattern looked out to sea. Scylla's six heads had been visible throughout their encounter with Circe, but she had now sunk below the waves again. Her underwater shadow was moving back and forth restlessly. Pattern pictured her pacing about on the ocean floor.

'I have an idea.'

CHAPTER TWENTY

Never trust entirely to your own fortitude.

S. & S. Adams, *The Complete Servant*

They made their preparations back at the house. A drowsy calm hung in the air, and when Nate went to check on the staff quarters, he found the rest of the menservants deep in an enchanted sleep. The building had always seemed like a Mediterranean villa masquerading as an English country house, but now the last of its disguise was gone. The only remainder of its former incarnation was the grandfather clock in the

hall, where the miniature figures of Miss Jenks and Mr Stokes continued to mark the hour.

Pattern began by visiting the gallery. The 'Home, Sweet Home' tapestry had vanished, but all the antiquities were still in place. She was chiefly interested in the red-and-black vase that had caught her eye on their first morning on the island. There was Scylla, all heads and tentacles on the front panel. But by turning the vase around, Pattern saw more of the story. Another panel showed a man embracing a young woman, while another lady looked on, a scowl upon her face. The next scene depicted a bird with lightning in its beak, and a towering wave that came between the lovers.

Pattern felt better for seeing this, the illustrations seeming to support some of her more colourful theories. Afterwards, she met Mr Ladlaw and Nate for a council of war in the kitchen. Most of its domestic trappings had been stripped away, and even a cook of Mrs Palfrey's talents would have struggled to concoct as much as a salmagundi salad in such a barren place.

At Nate's request, Mr Grey had produced a map

of the island. Together, he and Pattern pored over the various coves and inlets, before deciding that the beach with the stone pier was best suited for their purposes. Meanwhile, Mr Ladlaw sat and bit his nails. Mr Grey observed the scene from a haughty distance.

'We will need a large net too,' Nate said to the steward. 'D'you think you can find us one?'

'Scylla is not a *sardine*,' Mr Grey scoffed. 'I do not know whether to marvel at your optimism or pity your foolishness.'

'I have faced threats as powerful as your Lady and her creature before,' said Pattern quietly.

'A peevish housekeeper? A gouty steward? A butler who helped himself too freely to his master's wine?'

'A dragon.'

Mr Grey gave a bark of laughter. 'You, a dragon killer? I begin to see why my lady thinks you so amusing.'

Pattern squared her shoulders. 'Well, the dragon did not find me a joke, I can tell you. Moreover, I was placed in this household by an organization – a secret organization – that deals with such monsters on a very

regular basis. My colleagues have battled witches before, as well as ghosts and ghouls and all manner of demons. So, dragon slaying aside, I have been thoroughly prepared for this kind of emergency. That is why I have in my possession a chemical solution that can paralyse any creature for fifteen minutes at a stretch. We have only to lure Scylla within striking distance, contain her with the nets, paralyse her with the solution and recover the ring. Since the chemicals' effects are strictly temporary, Circe will get to keep both her monster, unharmed, *and* her love-token.'

Mr Grey looked entirely sceptical.

Mr Ladlaw, however, was very much cheered. 'But this is excellent news! Why ever didn't you say so before? You can use the rest of your potion on the witch, and then I can have a shot at her with the pistol.'

'For shame, sir,' the steward growled. 'My lady said she could see you as a raven; I myself think you would be far better suited to a weasel or a rat. Don't imagine you can hope to cheat and get away with it.'

'Mr Ladlaw will have every opportunity to redeem

himself,' said Pattern. 'After all, he will be playing an active role in our defeat of Scylla.'

'Yes indeed. I will be quite happy to carry any equipment and provide moral support.'

'We also need bait.'

'Bait?'

'Something to lure Scylla into our trap. She has no fondness for Circe's gentlemen guests, after all.'

'That's right,' said Nate with relish. 'Once she spies you out on the rocks, all trussed up like a Sunday joint, our octopus friend won't be able to resist swimming up to take a sniff of you.'

Mr Ladlaw began to protest very noisily indeed. He rose to his feet, and looked at the door. But Mr Grey put a heavy hand on his shoulder.

'My lady's eyes are everywhere. There is nowhere for you to flee.' His scowl turned on Pattern and Nate. 'That goes for you too. I said to the little maid I did not wish the island to take more prisoners. But it seems to me you have brought all your present difficulties on yourselves. I *told* you to keep out of my lady's way. I *told*

you she could not be defied. Yet you have paid me not a blind bit of attention! Indeed, for all your plots and potions, I think you had best get used to the idea of enjoying a *very* long stay on Cull.'

Finally, they were ready to go. Mr Grey provided them with a padlock and chain, as well as a bundle of fishermen's nets, and Pattern produced a flask of the solution that she said would render Scylla immobile.

'We only need to get her entangled in the netting,' she said, with as much confidence as she could muster, 'so I can aim a squirt in her eye. Any eye will do, so at least there are plenty to choose from.'

Mr Grey made another scoffing sound.

They tied Mr Ladlaw's hands behind his back for the look of the thing, and also to prevent him from making a sudden bolt for it. As an additional deterrent, Nate wore the pistol tucked into his belt. There was one bullet left, he said, menacingly, and he wasn't afraid to use it.

When they left the villa, the dawn mists had cleared,

and it was as if Cull was a woman who had aged forty years overnight. The island now bore the scars of a long drought. All its last traces of greenness and freshness had gone, burned away by the sun's relentless glare. The earth was sandy-dry, and the grass brittle. For the first time, the sky was overcast, leaden with clouds. The whisper and rasp of small insects was joined by a distant rumble of thunder.

By the time they reached the beach, storm clouds were gathering. Up close, the pier looked alarmingly high and narrow, and its end seemed much further from the shore than Pattern remembered. Mr Ladlaw had to be prodded along as if he were a pirate captive being forced to walk the plank. Waves rushed against the structure with a hiss and spit.

Pattern set about padlocking Mr Ladlaw's chains to a rusty ring used for mooring boats. She was not ignorant of the irony of the situation – in her last escapade, it had been her friend the Grand Duchess Eleri who was tied up as bait for a monstrous creature and, though she disliked Mr Ladlaw very much, she also pitied him.

'Be of good cheer,' she told him, as he slumped to his knees and stared out to sea in a despairing fashion. 'You only have to play along with our plan for a little while. As long as you trust me, and follow my lead, I give you my word all will be well.'

'You are a *housemaid*. You are a *child*. What do you know of anything?' Mr Ladlaw screwed up his face. 'I should never have listened to your fantasies. We are all of us doomed.'

His words hit home. Pattern could not entirely shake off the feeling that she was an imposter; when so much of her plan relied on speculation, so little was sure. Nate looked over from where he was holding the nets beside Mr Grey, and gave her a salute. She returned it as cheerfully as she could, all the while gripped by the notion that his faith in her was entirely misplaced.

Perhaps Mr Ladlaw was right, and she had deluded herself. Perhaps she *was* leading all of them to their doom. Either way, there was nothing she could do about it now.

She stepped in front of Mr Ladlaw so that she was

at the very edge of the pier. The wind whipped her hair, and salt stung her dry lips. Clouds were amassing overhead, swollen and dark as a bruise, and the sea was growing rougher by the moment.

'Scylla!' she cried out. 'Scylla! Lady Circe has a gift for you! Another treacherous male deserves your punishment!'

The wait felt as if it stretched on for hours, but in fact it was only a matter of minutes before a dark shape rushed through the water, churning the cove into a cauldron of bubbling waves. As thunder growled, and the sky pulsed with blue light, one of the waves twisted and turned in on itself, rising up until it was a high foamy column. The column plunged downwards, crashing back into the depths, and out of the spray of dirty foam a writhing knot of green tentacles appeared.

The tentacles twisted and coiled. Waves swelled and frothed. And then suddenly the upper body of a giant woman was surging towards the pier. Her skin was pale and glistening. Six long sinuous necks, as graceful as they were horrible, ended in six beautiful golden heads,

each bearing a smile of rotting savagery. On the hand of her outstretched left arm, a ruby ring flashed.

Mr Ladlaw let out a shriek of terror. Nate went deathly pale. Even Pattern, who had faced this horror before, felt as if her legs were about to buckle.

'There,' said Mr Grey with satisfaction. 'How can your puny nets hope to contain such an almighty force? Scylla will never submit to such indignities. She is invincible! None of your tricks are of any use against her.'

'I know,' said Pattern, and gave the signal.

Nate flung a net over Mr Grey and then barrelled into his waist, tumbling him to the floor.

'What are you doing?' the old man raged, struggling violently against the net. 'Get this off me! Impudent young lout—'

'You are right to think we cannot hope to disarm Scylla,' said Pattern as calmly as she was able. 'And so we have a different kind of bait in mind.'

Together, she and Nate unchained Mr Ladlaw and – with some difficulty – secured Mr Grey instead. Then Pattern pressed the pistol into Mr Ladlaw's trembling hands. 'Keep the pistol aimed at the old man's head.'

'Wh-wh-wh—?'

'Don't shoot, whatever happens,' she said into his ear. 'But you must act as if you mean to. Scylla has to

believe we mean business – and she knows that you, at least, have nothing to lose.'

Then she strode to the edge of the pier again. 'Scylla! We have Glaucus as our prisoner. Give us your ring. Your ring, for his life.'

The six monstrous mouths let out six wailing screams. The stench of rotten fish and weed was overpowering. The octopus woman was nearly upon them now, and her tentacles could have reached up and coiled round each of them in an instant, dashing them to their deaths on the rocks, or plunging them into the sea. But Mr Ladlaw held the pistol to Glaucus Grey's head, and Scylla hung back, lashing the waves with her tentacles and gnashing her fangs in fury.

Glaucus and Scylla had existed in the ancient stories of Ovid, stories Miss Smith had described as 'tales of betrayed love and transformation'. But what if these tales were no fiction?

'Here is what I think,' Pattern told Mr Grey. 'I think you and Circe were once in love, and she gave you a ring as a sign of her devotion. But then you fell for the charms of a girl named Scylla.' She was remembering the painted vase, one side of which showed two lovers embracing, while a frowning woman looked on. Then came the lightning strike, and the terror with tentacles. 'In the madness of your passion, you gave her the ring that Circe had given you. But Circe discovered your betrayal. As punishment, she turned your lover into a hideous monster, and made you her aged slave. Is this the truth?'

'Near enough,' said Mr Grey, and his voice trembled. 'It is certainly true that I did the first wrong. The tragedy is that we have *both* been punished for it.'

Pattern nodded. It was indeed a tale of torment, just like the stories Miss Smith had told her about.

'Then tell Scylla to give me the ring.'

'You won't hurt her? Your chemicals . . .'

'My flask of potion is useless. It is merely window-cleaning fluid. See?' And Pattern turned it upside down, emptying the soapy slops on the floor.

Glaucus Grey raised his head. He wore a rueful smile. 'Scylla,' he said. 'My love. My darling dear.

Forgive me, I beg. But please do give them the ring.'

Rolling purple-black clouds rushed over the sky with unnatural speed and strength. Lightning, jagged and blue, lit up the scene. A bird, storm-tossed, darted in and out of the roiling darkness. And Scylla howled and thrashed and lashed the waves as she tore at the ring on her hand and hurled it through the air.

The ring landed in a puddle by Pattern's feet. It was not made for human hands, but when she picked it up it shrank to an ordinary size.

Hot tears rained from Scylla's six pairs of eyes and joined the salt spray misting the air.

Glaucus Grey put his head in his hands.

A hawk swooped into the air around them.

'Very clever,' it said. 'Very clever, little Penelope. So you do know something of love, after all.'

CHAPTER TWENTY-ONE

A mistress will rarely have a servant from whom she will not gain some useful hints.

Mrs Taylor, *Practical Hints to Young Females*

Lightning tore through the sky and struck the pier with a blinding flash. There was an instant of white-hot confusion. Wave and cloud and stone tumbled together; the world turned inside out. When it was over, Pattern and Nate were standing at the foot of the summer-house steps. It was as if the storm had never been. The sea and sky were serene blue.

Circe was reclining on her throne, brushing a single hawk's feather from her hair. 'That was exceedingly well done. I can't remember the last time I was so entertained. My monster has been put in its place by my maidservant! Bravo!'

'Thank you, milady,' Pattern said weakly.

The animals had gone, so had the blank-faced gathering of women. There was no sign of Miss Smith or Mr Whitby, nor Mr Ladlaw and Glaucus Grey. They were quite alone.

'Are you sure I can't tempt you to stay and keep me company? The hall boy has also acquitted himself very well. I could train the two of you up! A brand-new butler and lady's maid. The three of us would get along famously, I'm sure.'

'No thank you, milady,' Nate and Pattern said in unison.

'We just . . . we want to go home with everyone else,' Nate added. 'Like you promised.'

'Well, well. I suppose I *did* give my word.'

Circe gave a lazy wave of her hand. The hill sloping

down from the temple was suddenly crowded with servants, including Mr Stokes and Miss Jenks. The party of ladies and gentlemen were among the throng, and Mr Ladlaw and Mr Whitby were joined by Lord Charnly, Captain Vyne and the Reverend Blunt. Everyone wore the same peaceful blank stare – except, that is, for Glaucus Grey. He stood behind his mistress, stony-faced. Out at sea, six golden heads bobbed about in the waves.

'It does stick in my craw to let the gentlemen off so lightly.' Circe sighed. 'They still have much to atone for.'

'It is small wonder you are so disgusted with society, when you surround yourself with those who embody its worst aspects,' said Pattern. She hardly knew what made her so impudent, but thus far Circe seemed to find her boldness a novelty rather than an outrage. 'Might you consider a change of project? Instead of punishing the wicked, you might reward the virtuous.'

'Hmm. Don't you find being so relentlessly worthy rather . . . dull?'

'You could try it yourself,' said Pattern in her mildest manner, 'and see if you like it better.'

The enchantress smiled, then shrugged. At once, the rest of the house party came to life. People looked about in mild bafflement, not quite sure how they had come to be out on the hillside, all mingled together. None seemed alarmed – except, that is, for the five gentlemen. Lord Charnly, Captain Vyne, Reverend Blunt, Mr Ladlaw and Mr Whitby were men still in the grip of a nightmare: limp and quaking and greenish-hued.

Circe beckoned them forward. 'Dishonourable gentlemen! You will not be able to speak of what happened to you here, however much it haunts your dreams. And if you commit new crimes, or fail to make amends for your old ones, you will find yourself on another of my island holidays. *No one* returns from a second visit. Is that understood?'

It was.

'As for the rest of you, your memories of your stay on Cull will be vague but pleasant ones. Those above stairs will praise the fine weather, liberal hospitality and pleasant company. Those below stairs will report easy work and generous tips. On returning to London, my household servants will be laid off. However, you will each be paid a year's wages in bonus and all provided with excellent references – except for Miss Jenks, that is. I cannot inflict *her* on another unsuspecting employer.'

Miss Jenks bowed her head. It was Miss Smith who spoke up.

'Please, my lady, but I don't want to forget my adventures here. I have enough material for several novels, and I would like to do justice to it.'

'I don't want my brain jinxed neither,' said Nate. 'What with octopus ladies and mad clockwork dolls, there ain't been a dull moment. I hardly know how I'll go back to just mopping floors and emptying slops.'

'And I have a report to write,' said Pattern.

'So you wish to remember me in all my splendour, do you? It's rather flattering, I must admit. Ah well. Since I am not due to return to these parts for another century or two, I suppose I can make an exception.'

Since the enchantress seemed so well disposed,

Pattern dared to push her luck still further.

'Pardon me, milady, but you did say that if I won the wager, you would release *all* the people on the island.'

'I told you it is too late for the other gentlemen in animal form. They have forgotten their human selves by now, and to turn them back would be a cruelty.'

Pattern swallowed. Her final request was the most presumptuous of all. 'I meant Glaucus and Scylla.'

Circe became very still. She looked at the ruby ring in her hands, turning it round, over and over. The aged steward stared fiercely out to sea, fists clenched.

'Well, Glaucus,' Circe said at last, 'you have been my faithful servant these many long years. So has Scylla, in her way. Perhaps the little maid is right. Perhaps it is time for your retirement. And so I forgive your betrayal, thank you for your service . . . and bid you adieu.'

She tossed the ring into the air.

Up it spun, twisting and turning, higher and higher, until it was nothing but a glittering speck in the sky. The speck multiplied, shimmering into mist.

The mist swirled down to envelope Glaucus. It

cleared for a moment, showing a man grown young and fair and vigorous, before sweeping him down over the sea. A golden head rose from the waves; two gleaming arms reached out to embrace him. Moments later, the lovers were lost in a swirl of rainbow dazzle and sea foam.

Just for an instant, Circe screwed up her face, in a way that made her look very old, and very tired, and sad. '*Now* are you satisfied?'

'Thank you, milady. You are very kind.'

'Then let us tidy up the place, once and for all.'

Languidly, Circe waved her hand. A little white flower sprouted from the ground by her feet and began thrusting rapidly upwards, unfurling velvety green leaves as it went. It was one of the snowdrops, or moly flowers, as Circe called them. More blooms appeared and spread, rapidly carpeting the ground with green and white. The air was filled with their swoony scent. In a matter of moments, the whole island was overrun with them. And as the last wave of flowers crested the last hill, the whiteness of their petals and the brightness of

the sun flooded together, dazzlingly. Everyone screwed their eyes up against the brilliance, and when Pattern opened them Cull was gone.

So was Nate. So were all the other island visitors, and animals. It was just her and Circe, on a snowdrop-covered hill, in the middle of the sea.

Pattern looked around her in bewilderment. 'What...? How...? Where...?'

'So,' said the enchantress serenely, 'it seems I must go on my travels again. But I have decided, after all, that I would prefer it if you joined me. A cunning little maid to replace my faithful old steward. Only think what fun we shall have!'

Pattern gaped at her.

'There are few things more delightful than immortality on an enchanted isle. You strike me as an adventurous type, so where in the world would you like to go? What point of history would you enjoy visiting? I can move through time just as easy as I can skip across oceans, you know.'

'Milady, I already have employment—'

Circe's sunny smile darkened. 'Take care, little Penelope. Your stubbornness is beginning to verge on insolence.'

'But you promised to let me go,' Pattern said helplessly. She, who had once been entirely alone in the world, now knew what it was to have true purpose, and a real home. And now this was about to be stolen away from her, all so that she could become slave to a sorceress. Never to be with Eleri again, or Dilys and Franz and her other friends in Elffinberg – never to see Nate! Never to make her report to the Silver Service, never to have another homecoming ... There were some things, she realized with sickening clarity, that were indeed fates worse than death.

She looked Circe straight in the eye. 'It was part of our agreement.'

The enchantress's face darkened further. 'Now you are boring me too. And you know I loathe boredom above all things.'

The snowdrops rippled beneath them, white as sea foam.

'I may have released Scylla, but I still have Charybdis, at least.'

Was Pattern to be tossed into the jaws of another monster?

'Wh-who is that?'

'My whirlpool.' Circe made a downwards spiral in the air with her finger tip. 'Though its currents are those that flow through time and space.' This time, her smile was dazzling. 'I will see you on the other side, little Penelope.'

In the blink of an eye, she was gone. In another, the ground and its frothing snowdrops dissolved beneath Pattern's feet, pitching her into the sea. She could not swim, and the weight of her skirts should have dragged her down in moments, yet instead she was carried aloft on the current that had begun to swirl round in a widening circle, like the watery vortex that had trapped Reverend Blunt. And, as with the Reverend, all her panicked chokes and splutters, her frantic kicking and her splashing, made not a jot of difference to the force of the waves.

Round and round she spun, as if the sea was a tub of dirty bathwater circling a drain, and the centre of the whirlpool a giant plughole. For the whirlpool had formed a funnel, a well in the water that was countless fathoms deep. And far below, at the base of that spinning chute, was the speck of an island, distant and glittering, like a star . . .

With every spin, Pattern was being dragged closer to the hole. She knew, instinctively, that as soon as the force of the whirlpool brought her to the edge of the funnel, she would plunge down to where Circe's island drifted on its tides of time and space. And then she truly would be lost, forever.

Something, or someone, grabbed at her arm. Something else grabbed her legs. Pattern tried to kick, but she was weak from struggling against the icy water, half blinded with spray, and addled with shock. Then her befuddled brain realized that this was no new attack – instead, she

was being pulled free from the relentless draw of the whirlpool. Already, the foaming lip of the funnel was receding from her view. Her rescuers were swimming against the current, and towards freedom.

Holding up Pattern's left side was the youthful Glaucus. Holding up her right was Scylla, restored to human form. Or not *exactly* . . . there were no tentacles or fangs, nor smell of rot. But the lovers' lower bodies were magnificent fishtails, whose powerfully muscular kicks were speeding them through the waves.

Pattern had barely croaked out her thanks when, with a smile, her rescuers plunged her back down under the water.

Was she to drown after all?

Salt water scorched her throat. Stars burst behind her eyes; her ears roared. Flailing about, she was churned and whirled by deep currents. She felt herself go limp as the black weight of sea pressed all around her, like a tombstone crushing her lungs.

Then strong arms dragged her back up again. There was a confusion of shouts and scrabbles. When Pattern blinked the water out of her eyes, she found that she had been hauled to safety by an angry-looking Cornish fisherman. She was on one of a little fleet of fishing boats that were making their way back to the harbour. A short distance away, on another boat, she could see Nate waving anxiously at her. In another, the ladies and gentlemen huddled together, looking somewhat green, and holding handkerchiefs to their faces to block out the smell of fish.

'How could you be so careless!' scolded Mrs Robinson, even as she tenderly wrapped a blanket round Pattern's shivering shoulders. 'To fall overboard when the sea is flat as a pond!'

Pattern stammered an apology. The other maids crowded round, clucking and cooing.

There was no whirlpool. No Circe. No Cull.

Or, rather, Cull was still there, but in a very different form. It was a windswept mound of mud and rock sticking out of a cold, grey sea. A fine drizzle, as is so

often encountered at the English seaside in March, hung on the air.

But then Pattern, glancing back at the island, saw a ray of sun briefly pierce the gloom. It lit up a patch of water, where two bright heads rose above the bubbles, and two pearly fishtails were briefly entwined above the surf. The only other person to witness this was Elsie.

'There!' the girl exclaimed in satisfaction. 'I *told* you Cornwall was full of mermaids and such.'

Epilogue

The more perfectly the apprentice fulfils his duty, the greater will be his reward.

S. & S. Adams, *The Complete Servant*

Pattern's report to the Silver Service was a long and detailed one. She tried to be honest about her mistakes, and explain her thinking as plainly as possible. Her account was more for the benefit of Mr Crichton and Mrs Jervis than Sir Whitby for, although the gentleman rejoiced at the return of his ward, he suffered considerable mortification over the

nature of Henry's predicament. To have fallen for the seductions of a mechanical doll was a stain on the noble House of Whitby. The sooner the unfortunate affair was forgotten, the better.

At least the young man showed every sign of leading a respectable life. His days of drinking and gambling were over; he devoted himself to archaeological study and the promotion of a vegetarian diet. It was rumoured the sight of a string of sausages or side of ham was enough to bring him to tears. By all accounts, Circe's other gentlemen guests were similarly reformed characters.

'. . . *So in conclusion,*' Pattern wrote to her dear friend Eleri, Grand Duchess of Elffinberg, '*it seems to me that Circe's crimes arose from boredom and changeability more than natural wickedness. Wherever she is now, and whatever fresh schemes she has embarked on, there is still a* small *chance her better nature will prevail. But I doubt she will ever truly mend her ways.*

How I am looking forward to coming home to Elffinberg! And, oh, how good that is to write! Your suggestion of a holiday by the lakes is an excellent one. I will be very happy to consider the problems of the education budget and the cheesemongers' dispute while we are there. For, as you know, days of nothing but idleness give me the fidgets.

I have just one more task to do, before I begin my packing . . .'

For Pattern had another note to write. She would send it to Nate's lodgings in Borough, proposing that they meet in Bedford Square.

She signed it 'Penny', but along with the note she enclosed a card. It bore the design of a feather duster crossed with a toasting fork. On the back of the card she wrote, *The first step on a new path?*

Acknowledgements

The author wishes to express her gratitude towards Miss Lucy Pearse of Macmillan and Miss Julia Churchill of A. M. Heath, for their immeasurable efforts on her behalf.

She also owes a debt of thanks to the worthy authors cited below:

The Complete Servant: Being a Practical Guide to the Peculiar Duties and Business of All Descriptions of Servants, by Samuel and Sarah Adams (Knight and Lacey, 1825)

Practical Hints to Young Females: on the Duties of a Wife, a Mother, and a Mistress of a Family, by Mrs Taylor, of Ongar (Taylor & Hessey, and Josiah Conder, 1815)

About the Author

Laura Powell, who may or may not be a direct descendant of King Arthur, was born in London, but grew up in the shadow of Carreg Cennen Castle in Wales. Much of her childhood was either spent with her nose in a book, or plotting to escape her hated boarding school. Having studied Classics at university, she now spends her time working for the English National Ballet and writing magical mystery stories. She lives in Camberwell with her husband and young son. *The Lost Island* is the second Silver Service Mystery, which follows *The Last Duchess*.

About the Illustrator

Sarah Gibb is a London-based illustrator. After landing regular spots in the *Telegraph* and *Elle* magazine, Sarah has gone on to illustrate Sue Townsend's Adrian Mole series, many classic children's fairy tales and even the Harrods Christmas window display.

Read on for an extract from

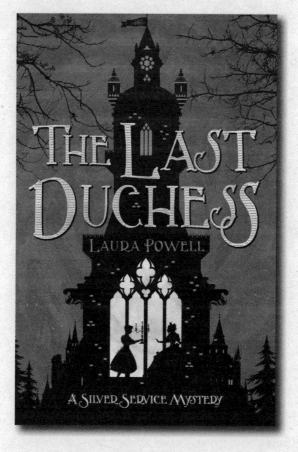

'An atmostpheric, intriging mystery'
Guardian

The castle lay at the end of a two-mile-long avenue carved through a pine wood. It was a vast and ugly pile, half Greek temple, half Gothic cathedral. Its ranks of pillars were stained by the droppings of many generations of pigeons, the tiers of windows looked as if they were rarely cleaned and the plasterwork was cracked and yellowing.

The main portico overlooked an immense cobbled forecourt and a fountain that dribbled water from a tangle of sea horses and mermaids. Pattern – naturally – was delivered to the back entrance, past stables large

enough to house several herds of horses, and into a paved yard where scraps of dead leaves and rubbish swirled. There she was met by a bootboy, who went to fetch a slovenly-looking maid, who went to fetch the head housekeeper, who went to fetch the master of the household.

All of this took a great deal of time, and Pattern, left to wait on the doorstep like an unwanted parcel, felt most uncomfortable. The master of the household, when he finally appeared, looked to have been roused from his tea, for there were crumbs all down his shirt and jam on his collar. He read the Baroness von Bliven's letter slowly and grudgingly.

'I suppose,' he said, even more grudgingly, 'you'd better come in.'

Pattern was passed back into the care of the Head Housekeeper, Mrs Parry, who was small and pursy, with shiny black button eyes. 'My,' she said, on first seeing Pattern, 'but you're a dismal scrap of a thing,' before asking her if England was as wet and dirty as everybody said.

Pattern replied that it was, on occasion.

'Well, I dare say one gets used to it. I doubt you'll be here long enough to get homesick, in any case.'

With these discouraging words, Mrs Parry informed Pattern that the Grand Duchess was indisposed and would not receive her until later that evening – if at all. In the meantime, she was to be given a tour of the service quarters. It appeared that a number of noble personages had apartments within the castle, and that attending to their needs provided employment for half of Elffinberg.

They began in the servants' hall, a draughty dungeon of a place filled with much noise and disorder. From there Pattern was whisked past laundries and larders, sculleries and butteries, pantries and spiceries; rooms for trimming candles, for storing root vegetables, for polishing silver and for blacking boots . . . Bells rang at every moment, from every corner, and people dressed in all manner of shabby uniforms hastened to obey them. It was an underground labyrinth, damp and dim as any cellar, though a great deal more confusing.

Pattern struggled to keep the pace, let alone remember all the information she was so carelessly and quickly given. She could not help but be concerned as to the whereabouts of her luggage, which had been taken off by the bootboy, and she feared the worst as to the tidiness of her hair and the cleanliness of her hands. Everything was so large and elaborate that she felt very small and insignificant indeed, and quite unequal to whatever tasks should be asked of her.

Finally a little pageboy scampered up to whisper in Mrs Parry's ear: the Grand Duchess was ready for them. By now, Pattern's throat was parched, and she was near faint with hunger. But there was no time for refreshment, let alone a moment to wash away the dust of the journey or re-pin her hair. Instead, she followed the rustle of Mrs Parry's skirts up creaking staircases with splintered hand-rails, along limewashed corridors and round cramped corners, through a baize-lined door that swung silently behind them – and into a spacious, well-lit hallway, with a carpet as soft as moss.

The doors to the Grand Duchess's bedchamber

were at the end. It was a room as big as a field, with a four-poster bed as a big as a cottage. The bed was walled with drapes of purple satin suspended from an enormous golden crown near the ceiling. Light glowed from a scattering of candlesticks; every window was shrouded in curtains of dusty plum-coloured velvet. It was stuffy and silent and seemingly deserted.

Mrs Parry advanced upon the giant bed. There was a set of portable steps propped against the end. Mrs Parry paused at their base, head bowed. She gave a small cough.

'Crumpets and crinolines! Am I *never* to have any peace?' exclaimed a peevish voice from within the drapery.

There was a sound of creaking bedsprings and flounced linens. The curtains twitched, and a small sharp face framed by a large white nightcap poked out. The face was scowling.

'It is the Young Person from England, Your Highness,' murmured Mrs Parry.

Her Royal Highness Arianwen Eleri Charlotte

Louise, Grand Duchess of Elffinberg, looked Pattern up and down and curled her lip.

'An English spy! How novel. I suppose they have run out of the native sort.' Then: 'Go away,' she said. 'Go away, both of you, and leave me alone. You make me bilious to my bones.'